Gover
Was Going

Groaning, Suzy dropped her forehead to the arm she'd braced along the edge of the sink. The battering that Gil's good name would take when news hit the streets that the governor had fathered a baby out of wedlock!

Slowly she raised her head. They can't find out, she told herself. If anyone learned of this, Gil would be ruined!

She gripped her hands on the edge of the sink and pulled herself shakily to her feet. No one knows, she reminded herself. No one but me. She stared at her reflection in the mirror. And no one will ever know, she promised herself as she went to pack her bags.

Dear Reader,

Welcome to Silhouette Desire, where every month you'll find six passionate, powerful and provocative romances.

October's MAN OF THE MONTH is *The Taming of Jackson Cade,* part of bestselling author BJ James' MEN OF BELLE TERRE miniseries, in which a tough horse breeder is gentled by a lovely veterinarian. *The Texan's Tiny Secret* by Peggy Moreland tells the moving story of a woman in love with the governor of Texas and afraid her scandalous past will hurt him.

The exciting series 20 AMBER COURT continues with Katherine Garbera's *Some Kind of Incredible,* in which a secretary teaches her lone-wolf boss to take a chance on love. In *Her Boss's Baby,* Cathleen Galitz's contribution to FORTUNES OF TEXAS: THE LOST HEIRS, a businessman falsely accused of a crime finds help from his faithful assistant and solace in her virginal embrace.

Jacob's Proposal, the first book in Eileen Wilks' dynamic new series, TALL, DARK & ELIGIBLE, features a marriage of convenience between a beauty and a devastatingly handsome financier known as the Iceman. And Maureen Child's popular BACHELOR BATTALION marches on with *Last Virgin in California,* an opposites-attract romance between a tough, by-the-book marine drill instructor and a free-spirited heroine.

So celebrate the arrival of autumn by indulging yourself with all six of these not-to-be-missed love stories.

Enjoy!

Joan Marlow Golan

Joan Marlow Golan
Senior Editor, Silhouette Desire

Please address questions and book requests to:
Silhouette Reader Service
U.S.: 3010 Walden Ave., P.O. Box 1325, Buffalo, NY 14269
Canadian: P.O. Box 609, Fort Erie, Ont. L2A 5X3

The Texan's Tiny Secret
PEGGY MORELAND

Published by Silhouette Books
America's Publisher of Contemporary Romance

If you purchased this book without a cover you should be aware that this book is stolen property. It was reported as "unsold and destroyed" to the publisher, and neither the author nor the publisher has received any payment for this "stripped book."

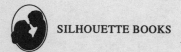

SILHOUETTE BOOKS

RECYCLED PAPER

ISBN 0-373-76394-8

THE TEXAN'S TINY SECRET

Copyright © 2001 by Peggy Bozeman Morse

All rights reserved. Except for use in any review, the reproduction or utilization of this work in whole or in part in any form by any electronic, mechanical or other means, now known or hereafter invented, including xerography, photocopying and recording, or in any information storage or retrieval system, is forbidden without the written permission of the editorial office, Silhouette Books, 300 East 42nd Street, New York, NY 10017 U.S.A.

All characters in this book have no existence outside the imagination of the author and have no relation whatsoever to anyone bearing the same name or names. They are not even distantly inspired by any individual known or unknown to the author, and all incidents are pure invention.

This edition published by arrangement with Harlequin Books S.A.

® and TM are trademarks of Harlequin Books S.A., used under license. Trademarks indicated with ® are registered in the United States Patent and Trademark Office, the Canadian Trade Marks Office and in other countries.

Visit Silhouette at www.eHarlequin.com

Printed in U.S.A.

Books by Peggy Moreland

Silhouette Desire

A Little Bit Country #515
Run for the Roses #598
Miss Prim #682
The Rescuer #765
Seven Year Itch #837
The Baby Doctor #867
Miss Lizzy's Legacy #921
A Willful Marriage #1024
**Marry Me, Cowboy* #1084
**A Little Texas Two-Step* #1090
**Lone Star Kind of Man* #1096
†*The Rancher's Spittin' Image* #1156
†*The Restless Virgin* #1163
†*A Sparkle in the Cowboy's Eyes* #1168
†*That McCloud Woman* #1227
Billionaire Bridegroom #1244
†*Hard Lovin' Man* #1270
‡*Ride a Wild Heart* #1306
‡*In Name Only* #1313
‡*Slow Waltz Across Texas* #1315
Groom of Fortune #1336
The Way to a Rancher's Heart #1345
Millionaire Boss #1365
The Texan's Tiny Secret #1394

*Trouble in Texas
†Texas Brides
‡Texas Grooms

Silhouette Special Edition

Rugrats and Rawhide #1084

PEGGY MORELAND

published her first romance with Silhouette in 1989 and continues to delight readers with stories set in her home state of Texas. Winner of the National Readers' Choice Award, a nominee for *Romantic Times* Reviewer's Choice Award and a finalist for the prestigious RITA Award, Peggy has appeared on the *USA Today* and Waldenbooks bestseller lists. When not writing, she enjoys spending time at the farm riding her quarter horse, Lo-Jump. She, her husband and three children make their home in Round Rock, Texas. You may write to Peggy at P.O. Box 2453, Round Rock, TX 78680-2453, or e-mail her in care of eHarlequin.com.

For Helen Heilmann, Janelle Shields and Vickie Monroe,
Kentuckians who took this displaced Texan
under their wings, offering friendship and moral support.
Thanks, ladies!

One

Gil Riley considered himself a simple man with simple tastes. He liked his jeans worn, his beer cold and his horses—as well as his women—gentle, but with enough spirit in 'em to make the ride exciting. Though his age placed him in a generation that shunned family values, considered work a four-letter word and embraced the theory "if it feels good, do it," Gil didn't quite fit the mold. He honored family second only to God, considered his mother an angel straight from heaven and his father one of the wisest men he'd ever known. He believed a hard day's work strengthened a man's character, treated women with the respect he was taught they were due, and never did anything without first weighing the consequences upside down, sideways and backward.

All of which made him wonder how in the hell he'd ended up in an airless room filled with blowhards, suck-ups and women whose mothers had obviously never taught them that a man's privates were just that. Private.

Duty, he reminded himself as he clasped a hand thrust his way and responded with a "good to see you, too."

Though the handshake he offered was firm and the sentiment sincere, Gil delivered both without slowing down. He feared if he did, and he was waylaid by one more person wanting a favor or had to dodge another female's straying hands, he would…

Well, he wasn't sure what he would do, but, whatever it was, he was sure it would be shocking enough to make the headlines in the morning paper.

With his smile feeling as if it were set in concrete and his tie like a noose around his neck, he set his sights on a possible escape route in the distance. He hadn't taken more than two steps in that direction when a beefy hand closed around his arm from behind and dragged him to a stop. Struggling to keep his frustration from showing, he turned to find a balding man, shaped like a whisky barrel and about as tall, beaming up at him, a horse-faced young woman hugged up against his side.

"Have you met my niece, Melanie, Governor? My brother Earl's oldest girl. Visiting here from California."

Yet another first-lady-of-Texas hopeful, Gil thought wearily. It was all he could do not to cry.

Thanks to his bachelor status and his exalted position as governor of the state of Texas, he'd received more propositions in the past year than a prostitute would in a lifetime on the streets.

Though he was tempted to tell Melanie that the rumors flying that he was gay were true, thus stanching any hopes she might have of becoming his first lady, manners and protocol—along with an ingrained sense of honesty—demanded that he extend a hand in greeting instead. "Pleased to meet you, Miss Melanie."

"Graduated magna cum laude from Stanton last spring," her uncle added proudly. "Brains and beauty in the same package. A rare find in a woman these days." The man gave his chin a jerk, setting the loose skin beneath it to flapping and Gil to wondering if he ought to duck. "Yessiree, a rare find."

Gil eased his hand from the I'm-not-letting-go-until-the-ring's-on-the-finger grip Melanie had on him. "Yes, it is, isn't it?" he replied vaguely.

Someone shouted his name from across the room, and Gil pushed his smile a notch higher and lifted a hand in greeting. "If you'll excuse me," he said, softening his smile to one of apology for Melanie. "I hope your stay in Texas is a pleasant one." With a nod to the woman's uncle, he turned and began to weave his way through the crowd again.

He reached the swinging door he'd spotted earlier and glanced quickly around to make sure no one was looking. Seeing his bodyguard approaching, he slashed a finger across his neck—his signal that he

was taking a breather—and pushed his way through
the door. Once on the other side he stopped, heaving
a sigh of relief, and the door swung back and smacked
him on the backside, knocking him a step further into
the room. But Gil didn't mind the whack on his rear,
considering it small payment to escape the pressing
crowd.

From somewhere he heard a woman's voice. "The
caviar's on the tray. Get it out there quick. And add
more champagne to the fountain. These pigs are swill-
ing it down faster than a drunk would a bottle of rot-
gut after a week on the wagon."

Frowning, Gil leaned to peer through a gap between the pots hanging above the long kitchen island.
The woman stood before a commercial range on the
opposite side, stirring a large pot, her back to him.
Balanced on three-inch platform sneakers dyed an ir-
idescent pink and with her white-blond hair anchored
on top of her head by a rhinestone clip shaped like a
star, she looked to Gil more like a refugee from a
punk rock festival than a member of any catering
staff.

Before he could make his identity known, she
dragged her forearm wearily across her forehead and
added, "Better check the supply of champagne
glasses while you're at it. It wouldn't occur to these
morons to simply ask for a refill. Oh-h-h, no-o-o,"
she said, sounding more than a little resentful.
"They've got to grab a fresh glass every time a waiter
passes by."

Finding the woman's sour disposition a refreshing

change from all the saccharine smiles and bogus compliments he'd suffered in the other room, Gil rounded the island. "You could've just tapped a keg, set out some plastic cups and saved yourself the hassle."

She whipped her head around, her gaze slamming into his. He saw the recognition flash in her eyes and prepared himself to graciously accept the apology he was sure she'd offer for mistaking him for one of the caterer's crew.

To his surprise, instead she turned her back to him and resumed her stirring. "If you're lost, the party's on the other side of the door."

"I'm not lost. I'm hiding."

She whacked the spoon against the side of the pot, set it aside, then crossed to the refrigerator, wiping her hands on a bib-style apron two sizes too big for her petite frame. "Well, hide someplace else. This kitchen's small enough without you in here cluttering things up."

Though her tone was anything but friendly, Gil decided he preferred her porcupine-disposition to the phony graciousness he'd experienced from the political elite gathered in the other room. Crossing to the range, he watched as she opened the refrigerator and stretched to retrieve something from its depths. As she moved, the back of her apron parted, exposing a cute little tush and well-shaped legs covered in leopard-print spandex capris. At the sight, he puckered his lips in a silent, admiring whistle.

When she turned from the refrigerator, he quickly dipped his head over the pot she'd been stirring, pretending interest. His mouth watered at the decadent scent of melted chocolate that rose to tease his taste buds. "Need some help?"

"Yeah, right," she said dryly, and shouldered him out of her way to add milk to the mixture. "Like the governor of Texas would actually stoop to scullery work."

Clucking his tongue, Gil shrugged out of his suit jacket and tossed it over a stool. "Just proves you can't judge a book by its cover...*or* its title," he added pointedly, as he loosened his tie. He tucked a dish towel into the waist of his slacks, then plucked the spoon from her hand and tipped his head toward the island. "Why don't you take that tray of caviar out to the guests before they come in here looking for it and discover my hiding place?"

She snatched the spoon right back. "My staff takes care of the serving," she informed him coldly, "and *I* do the cooking."

Gil lifted his hands and stepped aside, hiding a smile. "Just trying to be helpful."

"If you want to be helpful, you can get out of my—"

The swinging door banged open behind them and a young woman staggered into the kitchen, weighted down by a large tray of dirty dishes. She angled the tray onto the stainless steel island and blew a weary breath up at her bangs. Bracing a hand against the counter, she lifted a foot to slip her shoe off her heel.

"I swear, Suzy," she complained, "if you hadn't promised that I'd get to see the governor up close and

personal, I never would've agreed to work this gig."
The shoe hit the floor and she moaned pitifully,
squeezing her fingers around her aching toes. "No
man's worth this much pain. Not even the governor."

Another insult hurled his way. Gil couldn't remember the last time he'd had this much fun. "Are you
sure about that?"

The young woman snapped to attention, her gaze
meeting his, then quickly ducked behind the island,
but not before he saw her cheeks flame. Gil heard her
muttered curses and fumbling as she struggled to
squeeze her swollen foot back into her shoe. Seconds
later she popped back into view.

"S-sorry, Governor," she stammered, as she
smoothed her skirt back over her hips. "I didn't know
you were in here."

Smiling, he pressed a finger to his lips. "Shh.
Don't tell anyone. I'm hiding."

"Hiding?" Peering at him curiously, she rounded
the island. "From who?"

Gil nodded toward the door. "Them."

She squinched her nose. "I don't blame you," she
whispered. "Nothing but a bunch of browners out
there." She wiped her hand on her skirt, then offered
it to him along with a wide grin. "Hi. I'm Renee."

Taking her hand, Gil bowed slightly over it. "Gil
Riley, Renee. It's a pleasure to meet you, ma'am."

"Oh, for pity's sake," Suzy muttered, and pushed
her way through their joined hands, breaking the contact. She crossed to the island, grabbed the tray of
caviar-topped crackers and shoved it at her assistant.

"If you're done with the formal introductions, you can serve these to the *browners*."

Renee turned for the door with a long-suffering sigh.

"Remember," Gil called after her. "Mum's the word."

Bracing a hip against the door, Renee tossed him a smile and a wink over her shoulder. "Don't worry, Governor. Your secret's safe with me."

Chuckling, Gil picked up the spoon Suzy had abandoned and began to stir as the door swung shut behind Renee. "Cute girl."

"Hands off. She's jail bait."

Gil shrugged as a timer sounded, and Suzy headed for the oven. "Cute jail bait."

She shoved a tray of miniature pastry shells onto the countertop next to the range, then snatched the spoon from his hand. "Men," she grumbled.

Fascinated by this woman, but unsure why, Gil propped a hip against the counter and folded his arms across his chest. "You have something against men?"

"Nothing a mass castration wouldn't solve."

He flinched. "Ouch."

She tipped her head toward a plastic tub filled with utensils. "If you're staying, make yourself useful and hand me that ladle."

He retrieved the requested item and passed it to her. "Anything else, boss?"

"Yeah," she snapped. "Don't call me boss."

"What should I call you?"

"Suzy."

"Suzy...?" he prodded helpfully, hoping she would reveal her last name.

She slanted him a quelling look. "Just Suzy."

"Okay, Just Suzy. I'm Gil."

She rolled her eyes as she ladled thick chocolate into the shells. "Like I don't know who you are."

"Which obviously doesn't impress you overly much."

"Why should it?"

He could've hugged her for that response alone. "Why, indeed," he replied, smiling.

The timer sounded again, and before Suzy could stop him, Gil removed another tray of pastry shells from the oven, placed it on a rack to cool, then resumed his position at the counter, watching as she continued to fill the shells.

He had always thought a person's work habits revealed a lot about their personality and mood, and saw that this little lady was no exception to the rule. She tackled her duties with a confidence and an economy of motion that indicated she was no stranger to a kitchen. Yet he noticed a jerkiness in her movements and a tenseness around her mouth that told him his presence annoyed the hell out of her. She was also independent, he noted, zeroing in on the determined set of her jaw, the stubborn thrust of her chin, which told him that she was a woman who wouldn't need or want anyone's assistance...especially, it seemed, his.

But, dang, if she wasn't a pretty little thing, he

thought—if a person took the time to look past the garish makeup and the wild hairdo. Intrigued, he watched her hunch a shoulder to her heat-flushed cheek to brush away a wayward strand of hair and was tempted to help her out by tucking the lock behind her ear. But he refrained from doing so, mindful of her comment about castration and the number of knives within easy reach.

Wondering what had given her such a low opinion of men, he let his gaze drift to her mouth, pursed at the moment in an irresistible blend of annoyance and concentration...and found his thoughts shifting to wonder what she would taste like, what kind of response he could arouse from her if he were to give in to the sudden impulse to kiss her. If all her passions ran as deep and volatile as her temper, he suspected he'd be in for one hell of a ride.

"Do you work for the catering company?" he asked, hoping to discover her identity.

"I *am* the catering company."

"Should I be impressed?"

She glanced his way. "Most men are," she replied, then arched a brow and added, "though it's seldom my cooking that impresses them."

"Must be that winning personality of yours."

"That, too."

He tossed back his head and laughed, enjoying the verbal sparring. "So what do you do when you're not catering, Just Suzy?"

"Governor?"

Gil turned to find his bodyguard standing in the doorway. "Yes, Dave?"

"People are starting to notice you're missing."

Gil dragged the dish towel from around his waist with a weary sigh, feeling the full weight of his responsibilities settling back on his shoulders. "I'll be right there."

Dave touched a finger to his temple, then slipped back through the door as quietly as he'd appeared.

Gil picked up his jacket and shrugged it on. "It was nice meeting you, Just Suzy."

"Yeah, yeah," she muttered, busily plunking fresh raspberries on top of each filled tart.

Unable to resist teasing her a little more, he stepped up behind her and leaned to press his lips close to her ear. "If there's ever anything I can do for you…"

She jerked away, narrowing her eyes at him. "Like what? Washing my dirty dishes? Or did you have something a little more intimate in mind?"

Chuckling, he snugged the knot of his tie between the points of his collar. "Whatever your needs are," he informed her as he headed for the door, "just give me a shout, and I'm all yours."

With only a security light to illuminate the dark alleyway where the catering van was parked, Renee hovered at Suzy's elbow, worrying her thumbnail. "You don't think the rumors that he's gay are really true, do you?"

Remembering the governor's suggestive parting

comment, Suzy scowled as she shoved the last crate of glasses into the rear of the van. "Probably."

Renee's frown deepened, then she huffed a breath. "Well, I don't think he is. He just doesn't look gay, you know?" She sighed dreamily. "Oh, man, did you see his eyes? Paul Newman blue. And that drawl of his. I bet he could turn sex into a three-syllable word."

Suzy caught the door and stepped back, forcing Renee back, as well. "I thought your relationship with Rusty was exclusive?"

Renee gave her chin a defensive lift. "It is, but there's no harm in looking."

Suzy slammed the rear doors with a little more force than necessary. "Yeah, I've heard that line before," she muttered. "But usually delivered by a male caught with lipstick on his collar." Seeing Renee's wounded look, she immediately regretted the sharp words and slung an arm around her young employee. "Don't mind me. I'm just tired."

Renee's shoulders drooped wearily beneath Suzy's arm. "Me, too. Need me to follow you home and help you unload?"

"Nope. I'm leaving everything in the van until morning."

"You sure?"

Suzy hugged Renee to her side before giving her a push toward the parking lot. "Yeah, I'm sure. Now scoot. And give Rusty a kiss for me," she called after her.

Renee lifted a hand in farewell. "I will. Good night, Suzy."

"'Night."

Suzy watched until Renee was safely inside her car and pulling out onto the street, then headed for the driver's side of the van, anxious to get to her own home and bed. Catering an event of this size and importance was a physical and mental drain that took her days to recover from. Unfortunately, she didn't have days. She had a luncheon for the local garden club scheduled for noon the next day. Or rather today, she thought, stifling a groan as she stuck her key into the door lock.

Gravel crunched on the drive behind her, and she froze as a shadow fell over her, blocking the glow from the security light behind her. Silently cursing herself for not asking one of the security guards hired for the party to escort her to her van, she shifted her keys between her fingers and whirled, thrusting out her hand as if she held a weapon

The dark figure—a man she realized, gulping back the scream that rose—skidded to a stop with the blunt end of the key just inches from his chest and shot up his hands.

"Is that thing loaded?"

Though the man's face remained in shadows, Suzy recognized the voice. The governor. Furious with him for slipping up on her and frightening her, she dropped her arm. "Are you crazy?" she snapped, fisting the keys within her palm. "You could get yourself killed, sneaking up on a person like that."

He lowered his hands and teased her with a smile. "Would you miss me?"

Scowling, she wrenched open the door. "Get real."

He caught her elbow, stopping her before she could climb inside. "I'd miss you."

His voice was low, husky and sounded sincere enough to have her pausing…but only for the length of time it took for her to draw in an angry breath. Jerking free of his grasp, she spun to face him. "You don't even know me."

He hooked a hand over the top of the door and smiled down at her, his casual stance irritating her even more. "No, but I'd like to. How about dinner?"

"I've already eaten."

"A drink then."

"I'm not thirsty."

He shifted in front of her and pushed his palm against the side of the van, neatly pinning her between himself and the vehicle. He leaned closer and she drew back, wary of the seductive gleam in his eyes.

"Then we'll skip the preliminaries," he said in a voice that would melt the lock off a chastity belt, "and go straight to bed. Your place or mine?"

Suzy planted a hand against his chest, stopping his forward movement. "Neither." She gave him an angry shove. "Now beat it, Romeo, before I start screaming and have every cop in Austin swarming all over the place."

To her surprise, instead of becoming indignant, as she might have suspected, or using his greater strength to overpower her, he dropped his head back and laughed. Then, before she could duck, he surprised her again by dropping a kiss on her cheek. "I like you, Suzy."

Grimacing, she dragged the back of her hand across her face. "Yeah. Most men do."

He took a step back and slipped his hands into his pockets. "I'd like to see you again."

With room to move now, she climbed into the van and slammed the door. "Not if I see you first," she muttered as she rammed the key into the ignition. She gunned the engine, ripped the gearshift into drive and sped off, setting the glasses in the rear of the van rattling.

She rolled down her window as she turned onto the street…and would have sworn later that was the governor's laughter she heard chasing her down the street.

Gil stood before the windows in his office in the Governor's Mansion, his arms folded across his chest, staring out at the grounds below. Though late-afternoon sunshine spotlighted a neatly tended rose garden, he saw nothing but the scowling face of a flashily dressed, sharp-tongued blonde.

Thoughts and images of the caterer he'd met at the party the weekend before had filled his head all week, making it difficult for him to complete the simplest task and impeding his ability to concentrate on a particular topic for any length of time. Both of which were an oddity for Gil, as he couldn't remember a single woman in his past who had dominated his thoughts so completely.

Not that he hadn't had his fair share of female relationships, he reminded himself. He just hadn't met one like Suzy before.

Just Suzy.

A smile tugged at his lips as he envisioned her again, standing at the side of her van, dressed in those ridiculous-looking pink platform sneakers and leopardprint pants, brandishing her keys at him as if they were a weapon. She probably would have used them, too, if he hadn't spoken, thus revealing his identity. A hellcat, he thought, silently admiring her spunk.

"Gil? Are you listening to me?"

Startled, he glanced over at his secretary, then offered her a rueful smile. "Sorry, Mary. I guess my mind wandered."

She closed her day planner with a snap and rose, her lips pursed in disapproval. "And no wonder. You've been burning the candle at both ends since the day you took office. You need a vacation. Why don't you go to the ranch for a couple of days and relax?"

Though a trip to his ranch was appealing, he shook his head. "No rest for the weary. Not right now, at any rate."

"Well, there's nothing here that won't keep until tomorrow." She headed for the door. "At least go upstairs and put your feet up before you have to go to that meeting tonight."

"Mary?"

Her hand on the knob, she paused, a brow arched in question. "Yes?"

"Do you know who catered that party last weekend?"

She frowned slightly. "No. Why?"

He lifted a shoulder. "No particular reason." He dropped a hand to his desktop and shuffled a few papers. "Do you think you could find out for me?"

"Well, yes," she replied hesitantly, clearly puzzled by the request. "I'm sure I could."

He lifted his head and gave her a grateful smile. "Do that for me, would you? And give me a call if you're successful."

Suzy hadn't read a newspaper in years, avoided television newscasts like the plague and turned the dial if a news bulletin happened to interrupt the music playing on her favorite radio station. She despised the news, no matter what the format, and considered those who reported it lower than scum.

But her aversion to news and the news media hadn't prevented her from recognizing the governor of Texas when he'd slipped into the kitchen at the party she'd catered over the weekend. From the moment Gil Riley had tossed his cowboy hat into the ring and announced his intent to run for governor, he had become the most-talked-about man in the state of Texas. Within days of his announcement, his name and picture had appeared on billboards scattered along Texas roadways and on the rear bumpers of every make and model of vehicle, from the beat-up farm truck to the luxury sports car.

A nonpolitician—and a rancher, at that—running for governor was enough of an oddity to grab the attention of the entire populace. He quickly won the hearts of his fellow Texans by promising to represent the common man, especially those in rural areas, and put an end to big business and government taking over the Lone Star State and forcing families from their homes and off the land their ancestors had fought for and labored on for years.

But his platform wasn't all that caught the voters' attention. His youth, his Marlboro Man rugged looks and his bachelor status appealed to the masses as much as did his stand on the issues.

Especially to the women.

Throughout the months preceding the election, he was gossiped about and fantasized about in beauty salons, during coffee breaks and at the checkout lines in grocery stores. By the time November rolled around and his landslide victory announced, there wasn't a single woman in Texas who hadn't woven a secret dream or two of becoming his first lady.

Even Suzy.

And why not? Suzy asked herself with a defensive sniff. With his slow Texas drawl, his hard, lean body and that you-can-trust-me killer smile of his, the man was a natural woman-magnet. And if the stories told about him were true—which she seriously doubted, since he was, after all, a politician—he had more go-ing for him than just a handsome face and a to-die-for body. He was intelligent and possessed an almost uncanny business sense, with a degree from Texas A&M and a successful cattle operation to substantiate both. And he was a philanthropist, to boot, she remembered hearing somewhere, donating both his time and his money to causes that focused on abused children and troubled teens.

Handsome and with a tender and generous heart. What more could a woman ask for in a man? she asked herself.

Scowling, she rammed her wide-brimmed hat farther down on her head. "One who doesn't live in a fishbowl," she reminded herself.

With her knees buried in rich brown dirt, she kept her head down and her gaze focused on the weeds sprouting in her garden, telling herself that she wouldn't think about Gil Riley anymore. He was a walking, talking nightmare she didn't need in her life or her head right now or at any time in the future, no matter how attractive she found him.

But in spite of her determination to do otherwise, thoughts and images of the governor continued to drift through her mind as she worked in her garden, just as they had from the moment he'd waltzed into the kitchen at the party she'd catered, catching her unawares with his suggestion that she should've tapped a keg, instead of serving flutes of champagne.

Tapped a keg.

A smile twitched at her lips at the memory. But the smile slowly melted when a pair of cowboy boots moved into her line of vision only inches from her hand.

It can't be, she told herself, staring in horror at the tips of the custom-made boots.

"You're hard as hell to track down, you know it?"

It not only *could* be, she realized, recognizing the governor's distinctive drawl, it *was.* She forced a swallow, then was careful to fix a frown on her face before looking up. "What are you doing here? Hiding out again?"

"No. I came to see you."

His smile was as warm and guileless as the sunshine that beamed down on her face. But it was wasted on Suzy. She'd learned long ago not to trust a man's smile or be fooled by one's charm. She sank back on her heels and narrowed her eyes at him. "Why?"

He lifted a shoulder. "No reason. Was just in the neighborhood and thought I'd drop by and say hello."

She rocked forward, planted a gloved hand against the ground and started pulling weeds again. "Okay. You've said it. Now beat it, before I call the cops and have you arrested for trespassing."

Instead of leaving, as she'd hoped, he hunkered down opposite her, braced an arm on his thigh and dipped his head down to look at her. "Have I done something to offend you?"

She crawled to the next plant, refusing to look at him. "You're still breathing, aren't you?"

"Yeah, and obviously that doesn't please you." He

duck-walked to keep pace with her. "But what I want to know is why?"

With a frustrated huff, she fell back on her heels. "Is there a law that says every woman in the state has to drop at your feet and pant when you say heel?"

A slow grin spread across his face. "No. But if that's what it takes to get you to agree to go out with me, I'll see what I can do to push a bill through Congress to that effect."

She rolled her eyes and leaned to snatch at a weed. "Don't waste your time." He closed a hand over hers, stilling her movements, and she jerked up her head to glare at him.

"Look," he said patiently. "All I'm asking for is a little of your time. A chance to get to know you, and for you to get to know me. Now, that's not too much to ask, is it?"

"Suzy? Is that you, dear?"

She groaned at the sound of her neighbor's warbling voice coming from the other side of the privacy fence. "Yes, it's me, Mrs. Woodley!"

"Are you all right, dear? I thought I heard a man's voice."

She snatched her hand from beneath Gil's. "Nosy busybody," she muttered, then raised her voice, "Yes, I'm fine, Mrs. Woodley. Just visiting with a—" she glanced at Gil and curled her lip in a snarl "—*friend.*"

"Who, dear?"

Hissing a breath through her teeth, she scrambled to her feet and grabbed Gil's hand, tugging him to his feet, as well. "No one you know, Mrs. Woodley!" Dragging Gil behind her, she ran for the house. "I'm going inside now, Mrs. Woodley," she yelled. "Talk to you later."

Before the woman could respond, Suzy yanked Gil inside the house and slammed and locked the door behind them. Ripping off her hat and gloves, she tossed them onto the table as she raced to the window that faced her neighbor's house.

Gil chuckled as he watched her jerk down the shade. "I take it Mrs. Woodley is a bit like Gladys Kravitz."

She snorted as she darted past him to pull down the shade over the window above the kitchen sink. "Worse. And if she finds out the governor's at my house, she'll be on the phone telling all her friends. Wouldn't surprise me if she herded them all over to ask for your autograph."

He lifted a shoulder. "I'd be happy to give all your neighbors my autograph."

She sent him a withering look as she headed down a hall.

Shaking his head, Gil followed. "Are you going to pull every shade in the house?"

"You're darn right I am." In the living room she dropped a knee onto the sofa and stretched to grab the shade that partially covered the window behind it. She froze, then leaned over the back of the sofa to peer outside. "Oh, no," she moaned.

Gil crossed to stand behind her, stooping to see what had disturbed her. "What is it?"

She grabbed the string and jerked down the shade. "Not *what*. Who!"

Not having seen anything out of the ordinary, he straightened. "Who, then?"

She pushed from the sofa and stood, wringing her hands as she stared at the front door, as if she expected it to burst open at any moment. "Reporters."

"Reporters?" Gil moved to the end of the sofa and lifted the shade a fraction to peer outside. He glanced over his shoulder. "You mean those guys in that black sedan across the street?"

She gulped, then nodded.

He laughed and dropped the shade. "They aren't reporters. They're my bodyguards. Although Dave acts like an overprotective father at times."

"Are you sure?"

"Sure I'm sure." He opened the door and shouted. "Hey, Dave! Show this lady your ID."

The man behind the wheel lifted a hip, pulled out his wallet and flipped it open. Sunshine glinted off a silver badge he held out the open window. Gil glanced over at Suzy who had joined him at the door. "Satisfied?"

"They go everywhere you go?"

"Yeah," he said as he closed the door. "Well, not *everywhere*," he amended. "I *am* allowed to go to the rest room alone."

Suzy glanced up in surprise, then sputtered a laugh when she saw the teasing in his eyes. "Well, it's good to know that at least some things in life are still sacred."

"Do that again."

Her laughter dried up in her throat as she watched the amusement in his eyes soften to wonder. She took a nervous step back. "Do what?"

"Laugh." He caught her arm and turned her around to face him, holding her in place by her elbows. "I like the sound of it."

Heat from his hands radiated up her arms, setting off warning bells in her head. Though she knew she should send him packing, she found she couldn't move. But it wasn't his strength that held her in place, though she could feel the power in the hands that gripped her. It was something in his eyes. A warmth. A gentleness. And something in his voice. Warmth again. And a huskiness that made her toes curl inside her tennis shoes.

He touched a finger to the corner of her eye, and a slight smile curved his mouth. "And I like what it does to your face. It softens your features. Makes you seem friendlier, more approachable."

He drew the tips of his fingers along her cheek, and a shiver chased down her spine. "What…are you do- ing?"

"Touching you. Is that okay?"

Before she could reply, he placed a thumb against her lips and smoothed it along the crease. Another shiver chased down her spine as he slipped his hand around to cup the back of her neck. Her eyes riveted on his, her pulse thrumming, she watched the blue in his eyes darken, turn molten.

"I'm going to kiss you, Suzy," he said quietly.

Even as he offered the warning, he was lowering his face to hers.

And Suzy, God help her, was pushing to her toes to meet him halfway.

Two

Suzy knew one thing for sure.

Gil Riley sure as heck wasn't gay.

No man could kiss a woman like *this* and be anything but totally heterosexual. She couldn't think. Couldn't breathe. Couldn't move.

Well, maybe she could move, she decided belatedly and lifted her arms to loop them around his neck. The change in position brought him a step closer, his chest chafing against her breasts, his arms winding around her waist. With a skill that sent her blood racing, he teased her lips apart with gentle flicks of his tongue.

And forced her to add a new item to the governor's already lengthy résumé: master seducer.

He's good, she thought, giving herself up to the sensual rock of his mouth over hers, the erotic play of his tongue. Maybe too good, she thought with a shiver. Mesmerized by the pillowed softness of his lips, the commanding pressure of his mouth, she was only distantly aware of him sliding his hands from her waist to splay them across her buttocks. But when he tugged her up against him, she forgot about his mouth and the seductive lure of his lips, her attention snagged by the hard column of the erection nudging her abdomen. Alarm bells clanged in her head.

What are you doing! What is he doing! You don't need this kind of trouble. Get rid of him. Tell him to get lost. Toss him out the door on his ear!

She intended to heed the warnings. She really did! And would have, if he hadn't, at that moment, dug his fingers into her buttocks and lifted her, dragging her body up the length of his, until their groins were flush, their mouths perfectly aligned. With her held tightly against him, he deepened the kiss, softened it, then deepened it again, sending her pulse tripping, her mind reeling...and her good intentions skipping straight down the proverbial road to hell.

As he spun the kiss out, his tongue tangling with hers in an erotic dance for dominance, she lost all sense of time, all sense of place, all sense of self. She felt as if she were caught in the eye of one of Texas's famous twisters, her body battered by a constant barrage of sensations and emotions, her mind stripped bare of all thought and reason.

She wanted this man, she realized with a suddenness that made her heart stumble a beat. More than she'd ever wanted any man before, she wanted Gil

Riley. But even as her mind registered this need, he tightened his arms around her, all but squeezing what was left of the breath from her lungs. A groan rose from deep in his throat, and she sensed the regret in the sound, felt it as he eased his hold on her and let her slide back down his body, tasted it as he slowly dragged his mouth from hers.

Weakened, she braced her hands against his chest and drew in a shaky breath, telling herself that it was her imagination, that his kiss hadn't held the power, the perfection that her mind insisted on attributing to it. But when she opened her eyes and met his gaze, saw the heat there, the same surprise and passion that clouded her own, she knew she was in trouble.

He touched a finger to the moisture he'd left on her lips, and a smile curved one side of his mouth. "You're one hell of a kisser, Just Suzy."

And so was he, she thought, gulping. Before she gave in to the temptation to throw herself back into his arms for a second go at him, she inhaled deeply, drawing in the oxygen she needed to clear her head, steady her pulse and ease from his embrace. "You're not too shabby a kisser, yourself, guv."

He laughed and the masculine sound filled the room and vibrated through her, filling her with an unexpected sense of longing and regret she couldn't even begin to explain.

"I like you, Suzy."

Because she was afraid that she was beginning to like him, too, she turned away. "So you've said."

"My life isn't my own right now, but I'd like to spend what free time I can manage with you."

She closed her eyes, digging deep for the strength, the flippancy she needed to send him on his way. Plucking a pillow from the sofa, she slapped a hand against it, fluffing it. "Sorry, guv, but my dance card is pretty full."

"There's a private reception Friday night to dedicate a new children's wing at one of the local hospitals. Will you go with me?"

She dropped the pillow back to the sofa and turned, a brow arched in question. "This Friday?" At his nod, she lifted her hands. "Sorry. I've already got plans."

He stared at her a moment, as if weighing the truth in her refusal, then slipped his fingers into his shirt pocket and pulled out a small envelope. "If your plans should change, this will get you in the door." He dropped the invitation onto the coffee table, then touched a finger to his temple, his smile returning. "See you around, Suzy."

"What's this?"

Suzy glanced over her shoulder and swallowed a groan when she saw the card Renee was holding. Wishing she'd tossed the invitation into the garbage, as she'd intended, she turned back to the sink and continued to wash strawberries. "Some stupid reception for a new wing at a hospital."

"Are you going?"

"No."

"Why not? Everybody who is anybody is going. I read about it in Paul Skinner's gossip column. Even the governor will be there."

"So?"

"So go! Rub elbows with the rich and famous. Play Cinderella for a night."

Suzy snorted a laugh. "Yeah, right. Like I have any aspirations of being Cinderella."

Renee picked up the colander filled with freshly washed strawberries. "Oh, come on, Suz. Every girl dreams of being Cinderella at least once in her life."

Suzy followed Renee to the island, drying her hands on her apron's skirt. She picked up a knife and selected a strawberry from the colander as she settled onto a stool beside her assistant. "Not me. I quit believing in fairy tales a long time ago."

"Bull hockey."

Lifting a brow, Suzy turned to level a look on Renee. "I beg your pardon?"

Renee ignored her and continued to slice strawberries. "*Every* girl dreams of being Cinderella and meeting her own Prince Charming. Even *you*," she said, and stubbornly met Suzy's gaze.

Huffing a breath, Suzy resumed her coring. "Even if what you said were true, and it's not," she added, slanting Renee a warning look, "I certainly wouldn't find my Prince Charming at a hospital wing dedication." She sputtered a laugh. "Imagine *me* attending a reception with a bunch of snooty old do-gooders."

"Everyone there isn't going to be old and snooty. Remember? The governor's going and he's definitely not old. And he's not snooty, either. In fact, I think he's about as down-to-earth and friendly as any person could possibly be. And if there *is* such a man as Prince Charming,'' she added, ''Gil Riley certainly fits the bill.''

Before Suzy could argue the point, the doorbell sounded and the telephone rang at the same time. Renee laid down her knife and rose. ''I'll get the door.''

Hoping that by the time her assistant returned to the kitchen, she would have forgotten all about the stupid invitation, Suzy picked up the phone. ''Suzy's Succulent Sensations,'' she said into the receiver.

''Suzy?''

She squeezed her eyes shut at the quaver she heard in the familiar voice, recognizing it as a sign her mother was having a bad day. Determined to be cheerful, she tucked the phone between shoulder and ear, reached for the knife again and began to core strawberries. ''Hello, Mother. How're you doing today?''

''Okay…I guess.''

Suzy heard the self-pity in the response, but refused to fall prey to it. ''That's good. Are you planning to work in your garden today?''

''No,'' her mother replied in a lifeless voice that threatened to suck Suzy down into an equally despairing mood. ''I just don't have the heart for it today.''

''But it's a such a beautiful day,'' Suzy insisted, knowing from experience that staying inside with the curtains drawn would only darken her mother's depression more.

"Is it?" her mother replied vaguely. "I hadn't noticed. Suzy?"

Suzy heard the tears building and tensed. "What is it, Mother? Has something happened?"

"No. No." She sniffed noisily. "It's just that last night I dreamed your father—"

Suzy stiffened, curling her fingers around the knife's handle. "Don't call him that."

"I'm sorry, dear. The reverend, then. I dreamed the reverend called and wanted to see us. It seemed so real," her mother continued, her voice quavering with a mixture of fear and hope.

"You know what the doctor said," Suzy reminded her sternly. "You're not to focus on your dreams or to even think about them. You're supposed to occupy your mind on something else. Do you have any new books to read?"

"No." Her mother sniffed delicately. "I haven't felt much like getting out and going to the library."

"How about a jigsaw puzzle? I'll bet the new ones I brought you are still in the top of the hall closet."

There was a slight pause, and Suzy could almost see her mother turning to gaze vacantly at the closet door.

"You brought me puzzles?" Suzy heard her mother ask, as if she'd totally forgotten about Suzy's visit and her placing the boxes there.

"Would you like for me to come and visit you?" Suzy asked, her concern growing. "I have desserts to make for a party tonight, but I could come later this afternoon, after I've delivered them.''

"No, dear. I'll be all right. I'll just take down one of the puzzles you brought and work on it today.''

"Good idea, Mother. And go outside for a while,'' Suzy begged. "Being out in the sun and fresh air will do you a world of good.''

"Oh, my gosh! Look, Suzy! Roses! Dozens of them!''

Suzy glanced up, her eyes rounding as Renee returned to the kitchen, carrying a huge vase of yellow roses. Dumbfounded, she angled the receiver back in front of her mouth. "Mother, I need to go. I'll call later this afternoon and check on you, all right?''

"Yes, dear. That would be nice.''

At the click, indicating her mother had hung up, Suzy returned the phone to its base, staring as Renee set the vase of roses opposite her on the island.

"Aren't they gorgeous?'' Renee cried, laughing gaily. "And look! There's one sunflower tucked right in the middle.'' She quickly unpinned the small envelope from the ribbon wrapped around the sunflower's stem and thrust it at Suzy. "Open it and see who they're from.''

Fearing she already knew who had sent the roses, Suzy plucked a strawberry from the colander, pretending disinterest. "Probably some grateful hostess we catered a party for.''

"Then you won't mind if I look.'' Without waiting for permission, Renee ripped open the envelope and pulled out the card. She gasped, slapping a hand over her heart. "Oh, my God, Suzy! They're from the governor!" She lifted her head, her eyes wide, then dropped her gaze to the card again, and read, "'The roses are standard trying-to-impress-a-woman fare, but the sunflower is simply because it reminded me of your sunny smile. Hope to see you tonight.'"

Her cheeks burning, Suzy snatched the card from Renee's hand and stuffed it into her apron pocket.

Renee rounded the island, her mouth sagged open. "The governor sent you the invitation to the dedication?"

Suzy lifted a shoulder. "So what if he did? I'm not going."

"But you have to go!" Renee slid onto a stool, her knees bumping Suzy's as she spun to face her. "This is the opportunity of a lifetime! A date with the governor, for cripe's sake! The hunkiest and most lusted-after bachelor in the entire state. You'd be a fool not to go."

Suzy slipped off her stool, gathering the pile of cut stems into her hands. "Then I'm a fool." She crossed to the sink and poked the cuttings down the disposal. "Because I'm sure as heck not going *anywhere* as the governor's date."

And she *wasn't* going to the dedication as the governor's date, Suzy assured herself as she stopped inside the hospital's lobby to tug the strap of a high-heeled sling back over her heel. She was going to the dedication to prove a point...both to herself and Gil Riley.

They were totally unsuitable for each other.

She had known he wasn't the man for her from the moment she'd seen his picture on a billboard and felt the first flutter of attraction. That realization was confirmed the evening he'd slipped into the kitchen at the party she'd catered and she'd experienced firsthand his particular brand of heart-fluttering charm. And she'd had her nose all but rubbed in their unsuitability when he'd stood in her living room and kissed her senseless.

Yet, in spite of the obviousness of their unsuitability, Gil remained clueless...and persistent. But Suzy was willing to take whatever steps necessary to prove to him what she'd already ascertained, even if it meant possibly exposing herself to the public eye. Prior to going to the dedication, she'd carefully weighed all the dangers and convinced herself that she could conceal her identity from the unsuspecting guests. It was a private party, after all, thus the press wouldn't be present. Besides, she had chosen a disguise so outlandish, her own mother would have trouble recognizing her!

Straightening, she wiggled her hips to ease the body-hugging spandex fabric of her black micro-mini skirt back into place. She spotted the entrance to the new wing just ahead of her, and a smug smile curved her lips as strains of Mozart's ''Moonlight Sonata'' played by a violinist drifted out to her. She could just see the expressions on the faces of the stodgy, stiff-necked guests when she made her entrance. *She* knew she and Gil Riley were unsuitable…and, before the night was over, so would he.

Tossing over her shoulder the long tresses of the red wig she'd chosen to wear for the evening, she headed for the entrance.

"Excuse me, miss."

Suzy stopped and glanced to her right. A prune-faced woman stood at the entry, dressed in a pink slap-me-if-it-isn't-a-grandmother-of-the-bride silk shantung suit. Suzy arched a brow—the one she'd adhered a rhinestone to its end. "Yes?"

The woman lifted her chin, looking down her nose at Suzy in disapproval. "This is a private party, by invitation only."

"Yeah, I know." Hiding a smile, Suzy glanced over the roomful of guests. "I'm supposed to meet my date here." She caught a glimpse of Gil standing with a group of distinguished-looking men and looking positively mouth watering himself in a black tux and silk crewneck, off-white sweater. "There he is now." She lifted a hand. "Hey, Governor!" she shouted, waving her hand over her head. "Over here! I forgot my invitation, and this chick won't let me in."

Gil glanced her way—as did nearly everyone else in the room. Seeing this as the perfect opportunity to prove her point, Suzy gave the deep vee of her sequined halter top a tug closer to her naval—silently thanked God for double-sided tape—then cocked a hip and crooked her finger.

A hush fell over the room. Even the violinist

stopped playing. Though embarrassment burned through her as the crowd openly stared, Suzy kept her expression sulky and her posture slutty, holding her breath while she waited for Gil to turn his back on her, refusing to acknowledge her as an acquaintance, much less as his date. Once he did, she promised herself, she was out of there, point proven.

She watched him murmur something to the men he was standing with, then, to her amazement, he headed her way. Was that a smile twitching at his lips? she thought in dismay. By the time he reached her, he was laughing fully.

The prune-faced woman hovered nearby, wringing her hands. "I'm so sorry, Governor. I tried to tell her the party was by invitation only."

Gil looked down at Suzy, his eyes filled with amusement. "It's all right," he said, and offered her his arm. "She's my date."

Suzy slipped her arm through his and, unable to resist, tossed the wide-eyed woman an I-told-you-so smirk as Gil escorted her into the room and toward the buffet table.

"You really know how to make an entrance."

She looked up at him, all innocence. "An entrance? Me?"

He seared her with a look from the top of her trailer-trash hairdo to the tips of her scarlet-woman painted toenails. His lips quirked in a smile as he returned his gaze to hers. "Yeah, you." He unwound his arm from hers, picked up a plate from the buffet table and handed it to her, then selected one for himself. "But what I'm wondering is," he said, as he levered thin slices of smoked salmon onto first her plate, then his, "who you're trying to fool with that getup." He glanced her way and arched a brow. "Want to tell me about it?"

This wasn't going at all as she'd planned, Suzy reflected miserably as she fixed a smile on her face and shook the hand of yet another guest Gil introduced her to. Although she had succeeded in shocking nearly every person at the dedication with her trailer-trash hairdo and slutty outfit, her appearance hadn't seemed to faze or embarrass Gil at all. In fact, he'd treated her as if she were visiting royalty, insisting upon escorting her around the room and introducing her to what seemed an endless stream of people.

And if she'd had any clue she was going to have to march a country mile at the stupid dedication, she sure as heck wouldn't have worn these four-inch spiked heels!

Wincing, she braced a hand against his arm and lifted a foot to readjust the high-heeled sandal's strap, in hopes of easing the ache in her arch.

"Shoes hurting your feet?"

She glanced up, saw the amusement in his eyes and quickly dropped her hand from his arm and her foot to the floor. "No."

He bit back a smile. "Liar." He caught her elbow and guided her toward the entrance. "Let's get out of here."

"Suzy?"

At the sound of her name, Suzy stopped and turned, dragging Gil to a stop, as well. Her eyes widened when she saw her friend, Penny Thompson, hurrying toward her. "Penny!" she cried in surprise. "What are you doing here?"

Laughing, Penny grabbed her hands. "Me? What are *you* doing here?"

"I asked first." Suzy shifted her gaze higher, as a tall, handsome man stepped up beside her friend. "Don't tell me," she said dryly. "Let me guess. The Cyber Cowboy is a major contributor."

Grinning, Erik Thompson, Penny's new husband and the owner of Cyber Cowboy International, looped an around his wife's waist. "Okay, I won't tell you." He bent to drop a kiss on Suzy's cheek, then straightened, choking on a laugh as he got a good look at her attire. "I thought girls like you hung out on street corners."

Batting her eyelashes, Suzy sidled up to him and dragged a finger down the front of his tuxedo shirt. "Why, when all the johns with money are right in here?"

Penny slapped her hand away. "Watch it, sister. He's taken."

Laughing, Suzy fluffed her hair. "That's the kind of man I like best."

"I'll have to remember that."

Having forgotten all about Gil, Suzy shot him a frown as he joined them. "Trust me. It wouldn't help your case any."

Chuckling, Erik stuck out a hand. "Hello, Governor. It's a pleasure to see you again."

"Good to see you, too," Gil returned, then smiled at Penny as he caught her hand between his. "And you must be the woman who knocked Erik off the Most Eligible Bachelor List." He winked at Erik in approval. "An easy fall to take, when a man has a woman as pretty as this one to come home to."

Rolling her eyes, Suzy grabbed Gil by the sleeve. "Come on, Governor Smooth, before I'm forced to put on boots to wade through all this BS. Call me, Penny!" she tossed over her shoulder as she dragged Gil away.

When they reached the entrance, a man stepped forward, obviously one of the hosts for the evening.

"You're not leaving so soon, are you, Governor?"

"Not just yet. I thought I'd show my friend here some of the rooms in the new wing."

The man spread an arm in welcome. "Please, be our guests."

With a nod of thanks, Gil led Suzy to a bank of elevators. Once inside and the doors had closed, he dropped to a knee, and reached for her foot.

Startled, she tried to pull away. "What are you doing!"

He managed to slip off the left shoe, then glanced up at her. "Taking off your shoes."

He shifted to reach for the other, and she shoved at his head, tottering as she tried in vain to angle her foot out of his reach. "If I wanted my shoes off, I'd have taken them off myself."

He stood, dangling both shoes by their heel straps in front of her face. "No you wouldn't. You'd rather suffer the pain than take them off and destroy the image you're trying to project."

Pursing her lips, she snatched her shoes from his hand. "I'm not trying to project any kind of image."

"Yeah, you are." He pushed a finger against the crease between her brows. "Every time you take a step, you wince, a dead giveaway that you aren't accustomed to prancing around in four-inch spiked heels."

Though it was all she could do to keep from weeping with joy at the relief her arches were currently experiencing, Suzy refused to admit he was right. She folded her arms across her chest and stubbornly turned her gaze to the indicator marking their ascent. "It just so happens I *like* wearing high heels."

He moved to stand beside her, mimicking her posture. "Mmm-hmm."

She shot him a frown as the doors slid open. "I do. And as far as the personal tour goes, you can forget it. I'm going home."

She reached to punch the button for the first floor, but Gil caught her hand before she could press it.

"Later," he said, and gave her hand a tug. "There's someone I want you to meet first."

Suzy grabbed the edge of the door and held on. "I don't want to meet anyone else," she wailed miserably. "I've met enough old geezers tonight to last me a lifetime."

"This person isn't old." One by one he plucked

her fingers from around the door. "In fact, she's younger than you. And nicer, too," he added, as he dragged her down the hallway behind him.

Suzy's brows shot up at the slight. "I'm nice!"

"Mmm-hmm."

"I *am* nice."

He stopped before a door. "Did I say you weren't?"

"No. But you made that sound as if you didn't believe me."

He braced a hand against the door and pushed it open. "Mmm-hmm is a sound of acknowledgment."

Jerking up her chin, she pushed past him. "*Not* when you say it—" She skidded to a stop, her heart lurching when she saw a young girl perched up in the hospital bed. "Sarcastically," she finished weakly, unable to tear her gaze from the girl's shaved head.

Gil strode past her. "Hi, Celia." He sat down on the side of the bed. "How are you feeling today?"

The smile the girl offered him was weak, but filled with obvious affection. "Okay. What are you doing here so late?"

He took her hand and clasped it between his own. "I was at the dedication downstairs and decided to sneak out and visit my favorite girl."

She ducked her head, blushing. "I'm not your favorite girl."

"Yes, you are." He leaned close to whisper in her ear. "But don't tell Suzy. She thinks I'm crazy about her."

The girl glanced Suzy's way and smiled shyly. "Hi. I'm Celia."

It took Suzy a moment to find her voice. "Hey, Celia. I'm Suzy."

"Cool hair. Is it a wig?"

Hearing the wistfulness in the girl's voice, Suzy ran a self-conscious hand over her wild mane of hair. "Yeah." She took a step closer to the bed and wrinkled her nose. "Blew the minds of a few of those blue-haired old ladies downstairs."

Celia laughed softly. "I'll bet you did."

Suzy felt Gil's hand close around hers and glanced at him. He winked and tugged her to his side, sliding his arm around her waist as he turned his attention to Celia again.

"Have your parents been by today?"

The girl's smile faded and her eyes filled with tears. "No. But I didn't really expect them," she added quickly. "They both work, you know. Besides, they've got my brother and sister to take care of."

Gil squeezed her hand. "They'd come if they could."

"I know. Oh," she said, her face brightening, "I forgot to tell you thanks for the present."

She pulled her hand from his and twisted around to retrieve something from beneath her pillow. Turning back, she held a portable CD player out for him to see. "It's really cool. Thanks."

Chuckling, Gil drew his arm from around Suzy and picked up the headphones. He placed them over his ears and punched the play button. Wincing, he ripped them right back off. "What the heck kind of music is that?" he cried.

Laughing, Celia placed the headphones over her own ears. "Alanis Morissette's new CD. Cool, huh?"

Gil stuck a finger in his ear and wiggled it around, as if trying to restore his hearing. "It's obvious you have no taste in music. Next time I come for a visit, I'm bringing you one of my Dixie Chicks CDs. Now *that* is music."

"Excuse me, but visiting hours are over."

All three turned to find a nurse standing in the doorway.

Reluctantly Gil stood, then bent to place a kiss on Celia's cheek. "Hang in there, champ," he murmured. He gave her hand an encouraging squeeze as he straightened.

Gulping back the sudden flood of emotion that crowded her throat, Suzy backed toward the door. She forced her lips into a smile and waggled three fingers. "Nice to meet you, Celia."

Celia dragged off the earphones. "You can come to visit again, if you want."

The hopefulness in the girl's voice tore at Suzy's heart. She swallowed hard and nodded. "Yeah. Sure thing."

"I'll drive you home."

Still reeling from the emotional scene she'd witnessed, Suzy stepped away from the pressure of Gil's hand at the small of her back, anxious to get away from him before the tears that threatened burst out into a torrential flood. "I have my car."

He caught her elbow, stopping her. "Then you can give me a ride."

Over his shoulder she spotted his bodyguard standing at a discreet distance. "Dave can take you." She started to turn away, but he tightened his grip on her elbow, restraining her.

"Dave has other plans. Don't you, Dave?" he said, raising his voice loud enough for his bodyguard to hear him.

"Yessir, I do."

Gil shrugged. "See? What'd I tell you?"

Rolling her eyes, Suzy jerked free of his grasp and headed for the parking lot. "Is lying for his boss part of Dave's job description?"

Gil matched his stride to hers. "That wasn't a lie."

She kept walking. "Uh-huh."

"It's true," he insisted. When they reached her car, he took the keys from her hand, unlocked the door, then handed them back to her and grinned. "But he would've lied, if I'd asked him to. He's that loyal."

Rolling her eyes again, Suzy slipped behind the wheel and started the engine. "Men," she muttered under her breath.

Chuckling, Gil climbed in on the opposite side and closed the door. "Need directions to my place?"

She jerked down the gearshift. "Unless they've moved the governor's mansion in the last couple of days, I think I can find my way."

She made the drive across town to the mansion in

tight-lipped silence, while Gil kept up a steady monologue at her side. If asked later, she couldn't have repeated a word he said. All she could think about was seeing him holding the hand of that poor young girl with all her hair shaved off.

She started to make the turn onto the street in front of the mansion, but Gil placed a hand on the wheel, preventing her from doing so. He gestured to the rear of the property and a private entrance. "We'll use the back way."

She drew in a shuddery breath, silently praying she could continue to hold the tears at bay. "Okay."

She turned onto the drive, pulled beneath the portico and stopped. Forcing a smile, she turned to him. "Home sweet home. See ya, guv."

"Come in and I'll make us something to drink."

"Sorry. I don't drink and drive."

"Not even coffee?"

"Hate the stuff."

"Come in, anyway."

"It's late."

He leaned over and shut off the engine, palming the keys. "Not that late."

With her mouth hanging open, Suzy watched him round the hood. Wrenching open her door, she leaped from the car. "Give me my keys."

Ignoring her, he strode for the mansion's back door. "If you want 'em, come and get 'em."

Suzy stormed after him. "Give me my keys!"

He stepped inside, leaving the door open behind him. "Like I said, come and get 'em."

Fuming, Suzy balled her hands into fists at her sides, counted slowly to five, then marched inside, slamming the door behind her. She thrust out her hand. "The keys."

Gil merely lifted a brow.

She jabbed a finger against his chest. "The *keys,*" she repeated and turned her palm up expectantly.

Frowning, he braced his hands low on his hips. "What is it with you, anyway?"

"I don't like you."

"Oh, really? So I guess you always kiss men you don't like the way you kissed me the other day."

Heat rushed to her face and she quickly turned away before he saw it. "Yeah. I'm sadistic, so shoot me."

"You're not sadistic. You're a softy. And you put on one hell of a tough-girl show to hide it."

Furious that he'd hit so closely to the truth, she whirled. "Dammit! Give me my keys!"

"Nope." He took a step toward her.

Fearing if he touched her, she'd tumble, sobbing, into his arms, she took a step back. "Just give me my damn keys."

"I will...once you explain the tough-girl act."

He took another step, and she took one in reverse. Her back hit the door, and she pushed out a hand, flattening it against his chest. With her gaze on his, the tears that she'd kept banked since leaving the hospital surged to her eyes. "She's dying, isn't she?"

He hesitated a moment before answering. When he

did, his voice was low, heavy with regret. "Yes, she is."

. She squeezed her eyes shut. "Oh, God," she moaned.

"Suzy..."

Hearing the empathy in his voice, she stiffened her arm, fending off any attempt he might make to comfort her. She opened her eyes and gulped as she met the sadness and compassion in his gaze. "Who is she? A relative?"

He shook his head. "No. Just a patient I met while visiting at the hospital."

A tear slipped over her lower lash and streaked down her cheek. "You don't even know her, yet you bought her a CD player?"

He lifted a shoulder. "She likes music."

She sniffed and dragged a hand beneath her nose. "She likes music," she repeated, "so you bought her a CD." She choked on a watery laugh, then buried her face in her hands. "Oh, God," she sobbed miserably. "Then it's true."

"What's true?"

When she didn't answer, he caught her hands and forced them from her face. "What's true?" he asked again.

Unable to stop the tears, they streamed unchecked down her face. "You're a nice guy." Her breath hitched, and she slid down the door, sitting down hard on the floor, her hands still gripped in his, her gaze riveted on his face. "You really are a nice guy."

Three

Gil stared down at Suzy, baffled by the tears and how they related to what she'd just said. "Being a nice guy is a bad thing?"

Sniffing, she dragged her hands from his and dropped her chin to her chest. "Yeah. *Real* bad."

"I'm nice, and that's bad." He scratched his head, trying to find the logic in that association. Unable to do so, he dropped down on the floor beside her with a sigh and stretched out his legs. "I'm afraid you're going to have to explain that one."

She sniffed again, swiping a hand beneath her nose. "Good-lookin' and nice, too. Deadly combination."

Chuckling, he shook his head as he pulled a handkerchief from his back pocket. He dipped down to look up at her as he pressed it into her hand. "How 'bout if I start kicking puppies and stealing candy from little kids?''

She blew her nose, a halfhearted smile trembling on her lips. ''You'd still be good-lookin'.''

''I'll get a scar, then. A really ugly one. Would that help?''

She glanced over at his finely honed cheekbones, strong square jaw and blue, blue eyes. Even with a scar, the man would be drop-dead gorgeous. ''Maybe,'' she said cautiously, not wanting him to know how physically appealing she found him. ''Depends on where you put it.''

He tapped a finger against his lower jaw. ''How about here?''

She shook her head, the bump of his elbow against her arm making her even more aware of how close they were sitting. A stretch of the neck and a pucker, and their lips would meet.

''No. Here,'' she said, and reached to touch the high ridge of cheekbone. Unable to resist, she dragged her finger slowly to the corner of his mouth, following its path with her gaze, mesmerized by the warmth and textures she encountered. She bumped her finger over the fullness of his lower lip and she wet her own, remembering the feel of his mouth on hers, the weakness, the need his kiss had left her with.

A shiver took her and she glanced up…and saw that the teasing was gone from his eyes. He caught her finger, and she held her breath as he drew it away from his mouth. Almost wept when he leaned to touch his mouth to hers. Emotions, already exposed, were laid open, leaving her vulnerable, susceptible to his every move. Her chest ached with them, her throat swelled with them, her eyes filled with them. And when he framed her face between his palms...she was hopelessly lost.

She'd never experienced tenderness in a man. Never such deliberate gentleness. She hadn't thought she needed either of those things or even wanted them. But his kiss, his touch, produced a thirst she feared she could never slake, not now that she'd had a taste of it. If he'd asked, at that moment she knew she would have done anything he asked of her, surrendered her very soul to him without a moment's hesitation.

With his hands cupped tenderly around her face, he drew back and slowly pulled his mouth from hers. At the loss, she gulped back the tightness that burned her throat and forced open her eyes to meet his gaze. Heat simmered in the blue depths she stared into. The same heat she felt steeping behind her own eyes. But beneath the heat lay a veil of quiet compassion, promising so many things. Safety. Security. Understanding. Love? Were those the things she needed in her life? Were those the missing elements that kept her from feeling whole? Free? That kept her hobbled to an unsavory past and a family association she'd struggled for years to escape?

Too weak to move, too *moved* to speak, she closed her eyes and dropped her forehead against his. He's wrong for you, she told herself. Perfect, yet wrong. She drew in a shuddering breath, held it a moment, then released it slowly, trying to find her balance, her center, the strength she needed to move away.

But before she could make that move, he slipped a hand beneath her hair and cupped the back of her neck, squeezing as if he understood her confusion, her conflicting emotions, perhaps even shared them. The quiet strength in his hand, the comforting warmth in it, lulled her, and she let her mind drift, allowing herself to imagine her life differently. With a man in it. This man. Sharing moments like this. Laughing with him. Cuddling with him. Letting him love her. Permitting herself the freedom to fall in love with him. Such wistful thoughts, she scolded silently. Yet, sitting with him, his body a wall of strength and comfort against hers, it seemed almost possible.

The gentle squeeze of his fingers on her nape finally drew her back to the present, their place on the floor. Had seconds passed? Hours? She didn't know. Didn't care. She knew only that she wanted to hang on to this moment, remain this way with him forever.

But she couldn't. Not with Gil Riley. Not if she wanted to maintain her privacy, protect her identity. Not if she wanted to keep her past tucked safely away.

Digging deep for the willpower she needed to separate herself from him, she lifted her head.

And he smiled.

He didn't say anything, do anything, demand anything of her. He simply smiled that soft, heart-melting smile of his.

"I like you, Suzy."

Though she tried, she couldn't tear her gaze from his. "So you've said."

He tightened his fingers at her neck and drew her face toward his, the smile tugging the curve of his lips higher. "Have I?"

"Ye-es."

He touched his mouth to hers, and she squeezed her eyes shut against the need that swelled inside her.

He withdrew to nip at her lower lip. "I hate it when I'm redundant."

Though everything within her cried out for her to throw her arms around this man and hold on tight, she pressed a hand firmly against his chest, forcing him back even further. Her mouth went dry at the handsomeness of his features, the heat she found in his eyes. Knowing she had to do something to end this before he managed to seduce her completely, she wet her lips. "M-maybe I'll take that drink, after all."

Thirty minutes later they were sitting on the floor again, this time in the upstairs den of Gil's private quarters. They sat side by side, their shoulders touching, their backs braced against the sofa, both staring at the empty fireplace, lost for the moment in their own private thoughts.

Suzy didn't know what thoughts filled Gil's mind, but hers were focused on him, trying to decide how much of him was hype and how much was real. She knew all too well that an image could be created and projected totally opposite of—or at least masking—a person's true self. Hadn't she created one for herself?

Hadn't she learned the method from the master of mask wearers himself, her own father, who had used his mask to selfishly garner money and power?

Troubled by that thought, the possible similarities in personalities between her father and Gil, she slid a sideways glance at him. "Did you always want to be governor?"

He snorted and shook his head. "Hardly."

"Then why did you run?"

He moved his shoulder against hers in a shrug. "Duty more than anything, I guess."

"Duty?"

He drew up a leg and rested his arm on it, dangling his wineglass over his knee, his gaze still on the empty fireplace. "Someone had to stand up for the common man. Why not me?"

"Do you have higher aspirations?"

He glanced her way. "Like what?"

"Senator. President."

"Hell, no," he said with a shudder.

She continued to study him while sipping her wine, looking for a crack in the mask, any indication that he was lying. When she found none, she shook her head and turned her gaze back to the fireplace. "Weird."

"What's weird?"

"You."

"What makes you say that?"

"You're a politician. All politicians aspire to a greater office, more power."

He pulled his index finger away from his glass and aimed it at her. "I'm *not* a politician."

"Sure you are. You're the governor, aren't you?"

"For the next three years. But then it's over. When my term ends, I'm hightailing it back to my ranch."

Surprised by the fervor of his response, she scooted around to face him. "You sound as if you don't really enjoy being governor."

"I don't."

"Then why did you run?"

"Duty."

"You said that already. Duty to *whom?*"

"The common man. The rancher, the farmer, the small businessman. It was way past time someone stood up for them, pushed for legislation in their favor for a change."

"And you felt it was your responsibility to take that stand for them?"

"Not just for them. For me, too. I'm one of 'em. What affects them, affects me."

She clasped her hands dramatically over her heart. "The white knight, charging in to save the damsel in distress. The town marshal, dedicated to bringing law and order to the Wild West." Chuckling, she shook her head at the grand and selfless images his explanation had drawn. "Surely you must have a few vices?"

Smiling, he rolled to his side and stretched out an arm along the sofa behind her. "One." He nipped at her bare shoulder. "I have a weakness for smart-mouthed blondes with an attitude. Especially ones who wear red wigs.''

Laughing, she pushed at his head. ''Get outta here.''

He drew back, holding up a hand. ''Scout's honor. My heart goes pitter-patter every time I think about you.''

''Pitter-patter?'' she repeated, then laughed again.

He touched a finger to her lips...and her laughter dried up in her throat. He looked so serious, so awed...by her?

''What?'' she asked, uncomfortable with the intensity of his gaze.

''Your laugh. I like hearing it.'' He leaned to brush his lips across hers. ''Makes my heart smile.''

And he made her heart all but *stop*. With his kisses, with all his sweet-talk. And that scared the holy hell out of her. ''Maybe I should take my act on the road.''

He withdrew slightly, drawing his brows together. ''Why do you do that?''

''Do what?''

''When things begin to get intimate, you always make some sarcastic remark.''

''Do I?'' She knew damn good and well she did. She'd worked for years perfecting the technique.

''Yeah, you do.''

She batted her eyelashes at him. ''I guess it's just part of my irresistible charm.''

He laughed, then leaned to kiss her. ''I don't know why I find you so irresistible, but for some damn reason I do.'' He opened his mouth more fully over hers and stole her breath. ''And you know what else?'' he murmured, dragging a hand down her arm.

''What?''

''I want to make love with you.''

She placed a restraining a hand on his chest. ''Gil—''

Before she could say more, he captured her mouth completely, silencing her. Slowly he drew back to press a finger across the moisture he'd left on her lips. ''I've wanted to make love to you since the first night we met.'' He lifted his gaze to hers, and she found the earnestness of his expression as debilitating and arousing as his lips, his voice. ''You're all I think about. All I *want* to think about. And that really chaps me, because no woman has ever had that effect on me before.''

''Gil—''

''There's something right about us,'' he continued, refusing to let her speak. ''Something clicks when we're together. When I hold you or kiss you—'' Groaning, he caught her hand and dragged it down his chest, pressing it against the column of flesh that tented his slacks, showing her the effect she had on him.

''I want to make love to you, Suzy,'' he said again, his voice huskier now, more insistent. ''I need to know if this is just lust…or something more.''

With her hand held against the length and growing hardness of his erection, she could only stare, her body trembling, moved beyond words by his confession, by his obvious arousal, yet at the same time terrified by it all. She wanted to believe that he was lying, that he was simply delivering a polished line he used to lure women into his bed.

But something in his eyes told her that he wasn't lying. There was a sincerity beneath the heat that told her he spoke only the truth. Something, too, that warned her he wasn't the kind of man who considered sex a sport. This wouldn't be a casual falling in and out of bed for Gil Riley. He would give himself totally to an affair, as he did to everything he undertook, and would expect nothing less in return.

And that's what frightened Suzy, twisted her stomach into knots. She'd never given herself totally to anything or anyone before. And most certainly never a man.

She wet her lips and forced a swallow. "And if it's not just lust?"

He drew her hand back to his chest and fisted it against his heart. "What if it is?"

But what if it's not! she cried inwardly. She couldn't allow herself to fall in love with Gil Riley. Any kind of relationship with him would be insane, self-destructive, potentially suicidal. She hated the media, avoided it at all costs, and he lived out his life on the front page every day. He was a cowboy, and she was…well, she was just Suzy, a free spirit, a woman who changed her hair color and style to suit her mood, a woman who chose her wardrobe for its shock value, rather than for its suitability or practicality.

But as she continued to stare into his eyes, her palm recording every thunderous beat of his heart, she could only come up with one reason why she *shouldn't* refuse him.

She wanted to make love with him. And nothing, no matter how great the risk, could stop her from doing so, if only just this one time.

Knowing that, she leaned into him, found his mouth with hers and gave him the answer she didn't have the courage to voice.

At her surrender, he slipped a hand beneath her hips and hauled her across his lap. He quickly took the kiss deeper, the pace faster, the heat higher until she was all but blinded by it. The gentleness and tenderness she'd discovered and appreciated in him earlier was gone, but she decided she preferred the urgency, the desperation she tasted in him now, and matched it with an impatience of her own.

She felt his hands roaming her hips, smoothing down her legs, then back up, pushing her skirt higher on her thighs and her breath from her lungs. She felt him slip a finger beneath the elastic of her panties and gasped as he found her center. She groaned low in her throat, the sound echoing in her mind, as he slid a finger into her honeyed opening. The heat became unbearable, the need to have him inside her an obsession that took control of her mind and hands, her very soul.

Her movements frenetic, she shoved his jacket from his shoulders, then tugged his sweater from his slacks, whimpering her frustration at the awkwardness of their positions until he joined in her struggle to free him of his clothes. With his chest at last bare beneath her hands, she tore her mouth from his and pushed back on his lap. "I want you," she said, gulping for air as she reached for his belt buckle. "Now."

He worked with her to shove his slacks and underwear to his knees. "Do I need protection?"

She ripped off her panties and sent them flying across the room. "No. I'm on the pill." She jacked her skirt to her waist as she shifted to straddle him, then lifted her gaze to his and pressed a finger against his lips. "Lust," she told him, as she lowered herself down. "Lust," she repeated more determinedly, then tensed, gasping, when he lifted his hips to meet her.

With one smooth thrust, he buried himself inside her. She dropped her head back on a sob and dug her nails deeply into his shoulders as her body convulsed violently around him. He pushed deeper and, on a strangled cry, she clamped her thighs at his hips, his name a silent scream through her mind as pleasure ripped through her body like jagged bolts of lightning across a dark, summer sky.

Desperate to share with him the pleasure, she inhaled deeply, then raised her hips, drawing him out, until only the tip of his sex joined them. "Lust," she said again, as she lowered herself and began to ride him. "Lust," she all but sobbed, as he thrust harder and faster, pushing her over the edge again and again, until her climax seemed a continuous spasm of blinding pleasure.

Breathless and trembling, she clung to him, fearing

she would shatter if she lost her grip. And when he reached his own climax, his hands gripped tightly at her hips, holding her against him, his seed filling her, she could only cling more desperately, stunned by the sensations and emotions that rocked her, tears of both joy and regret pushing at her throat and stinging her eyes.

Still numbed by what she'd experienced, Suzy watched Gil reach for his slacks.

"Lust," she said, as if by voicing the word aloud she could convince herself that what they'd just shared was a temporary emotion, one they'd satisfied once and for all with their frenzied, if fantastic, love-making.

"I don't know," he replied doubtfully.

Her eyes rounded. "You don't know," she repeated, feeling the panic rising to squeeze at her chest.

"If it were just lust, I don't think I'd already be plotting ways to throw you down on the sofa and make love with you again, do you?"

Suzy glanced at the sofa, gulping as she imagined them there, their bodies tangled and slick with perspiration, their hips melded, their bodies joined intimately. "I don't know. You might."

"Well, since we're both unsure, I think we should give this a little more time before we make a final determination. Let's go to my ranch."

It took a moment for the unexpected invitation to sink in. She snapped her head around to stare at him in surprise. "Go to your ranch?"

Seeming to warm to the idea, he pulled up his zipper. "Yeah. I was planning on asking you to go with me tomorrow, anyway, but if we leave tonight, it'll give us two full days there together."

"I don't know," she replied hesitantly.

Smiling, he slipped his arms around her waist and tugged her hips up against his. "Come on, Suzy," he coaxed as he bent his head to nuzzle her neck. "It'll be fun. A relaxing weekend at the ranch, with nothing to do and no one to bother us." He lifted his head, his expression and his voice both filled with boyish pleading. "Please? It'll give us a chance to work on our lust theory some more."

Two full days alone with Gil Riley with unlimited sex? Still flushed from their last lovemaking session, she wanted to scream *yes* at the top of her lungs, but visions of a wagon train of news media trailing their every step made her continue to hesitate.

"If you're worried about the media knowing we're there," he added, as if reading her mind, "they won't. My ranch is remote, and night offers us the perfect cover to get there undetected."

"How can you be sure?" she asked, feeling herself weakening.

He gave her a confident smile. "Trust me. I just know."

She caught her lower lip between her teeth, knowing she should refuse him, but knowing, too, that she wanted to go. A weekend, she told herself. Really only two days, when she considered that it was presently the middle of the night. "I'll need to go home and pack a bag."

"Why?"

Exasperated, she held out her arms. "I can't very well run around all weekend dressed like *this*."

He rubbed his groin suggestively against her. "To be honest, I was hoping you wouldn't be wearing anything at all."

Heat poured through her bloodstream at his suggestion, at the feel of his arousal rubbing against her groin. "But I'll need my toothbrush," she insisted stubbornly, struggling to remain sensible, rational.

"No, you won't." He dipped his head over hers, his lips curving against hers in a smile. "I keep an extra set of toiletries on hand, in case of emergencies such as this."

It occurred to Suzy to ask if those emergencies were always of a female nature, but then he opened his mouth completely over hers, stealing her breath and emptying her mind, and she couldn't think at all.

He released her with a reluctant groan, then tucked a shoulder into her midsection and lifted her off her feet.

She grabbed for his belt. "Gil!" she squealed. "What are you doing!"

"Carrying you."

"Put me down, you ignoramus, before you drop me!"

He locked an arm over the back of her knees and headed for the door. "Uh-uh-uh," he scolded. "No name calling."

She grabbed for the door frame as he passed through the opening, but her fingers slipped from the jamb.

"Gil!" she screamed, her head bumping wildly against his back as he loped down the stairs. "You're going to crack my skull!"

"Governor?"

Gil skidded to a stop on the landing and looked over the banister to the hallway below. "What is it, Dave?"

Suzy moaned pitifully, just imagining the view of her backside Dave was receiving. "Put me down!" she hissed at Gil.

"Is everything okay up there?" Dave called.

Gil bent over and planted Suzy on her feet. "Everything's fine. We were just horsing around."

Glaring at Gil, Suzy jerked her skirt back over her hips, then turned and forced a pleasant smile to her face. "Hello, Dave."

He grinned up at her. "Hi. Having fun?"

"Oh, tons," she said dryly.

Gil slung an arm around her shoulders and started her down the stairs. "We were just leaving for the ranch."

Dave glanced at Suzy, his surprise obvious, then quickly turned away. "It'll only take me a minute to get my things."

Reaching the doorway to the kitchen, Gil ushered Suzy through it. "Take the weekend off, Dave," he called to his bodyguard, stopping him. Winking, he lifted a hand in a wave. "See you Monday."

* * *

Suzy awakened to darkness and a strange—and empty—bed. Blinking sleepily, she pushed up to her elbows and glanced around, looking for Gil. Across the room the patio door stood ajar. Wondering if he'd gone outside, she scooted off the bed and padded across the room. With her arms hugged across her bare breasts, she paused in the doorway and found him sitting in a willow chair, his back to her, naked as the day he was born.

As if sensing her presence, he held out a hand. "Come watch the sunrise with me. It's a sight to behold from this spot."

Her heart melting at the sweetness of the invitation, the ease he obviously felt with her, she crossed to him and placed her hand in his. He glanced up, smiled, then drew her down across his lap.

Content, she snuggled against his chest and looked around. The stone patio spread fan-like twelve feet or more from the bedroom door. Scattered about the smooth flagstones were clay pots filled with plants unidentifiable in the darkness and a matching willow chair next to the one which they shared. In the distance, oak trees stood like towering sentinels at the perimeter of the yard. Beyond them she could just make out the shape of pipe fencing, and beyond that, a dark sea of grass, the dew on the gently swaying blades gleaming like diamonds in the fading moonlight.

And cloaking it all was a peacefulness, a quiet serenity so pure it brought tears to her eyes.

"It's beautiful out here," she whispered, in deference to the stillness.

He tightened his arms around her and drew her closer to his chest. "Yeah, it is."

"Have you lived here long?"

"All my life."

She glanced up, hearing the pride in the simple answer, the satisfaction, then looked over his shoulder. "But the house looks almost new," she said in confusion.

"I meant on the ranch, not in this particular house."

"Oh."

Chuckling softly, he hugged her to him, and the sound rumbled against her ribs, drawing a smile to her lips and to her heart. She settled back against him.

"But you're right," he said. "The house is fairly new. I had it built about five years ago."

She turned her head to peer over his shoulder again, curious about his home. She hadn't been able to tell much about the house the night before. They'd arrived late and gone straight to his room and to bed...though not necessarily to sleep, she remembered.

Warmed by the memory of their lovemaking, she turned to look at him again and reached to lay a hand against his cheek. A night's growth of beard scraped her palm, the line of jaw she traced her fingers along straight and strong. A man's man, she thought, admiring the strength in his shadowed profile. A man who would never run from danger, one who would fight for justice and fairness for all. One who would find satisfaction in working with the land and who was more than capable of meeting whatever challenges it presented.

Sighing, she let her hand drop to cover his at her waist and tucked her head beneath his chin, her thoughts dreamy as she joined her gaze with his to stare at the gray-pink sky. A tiny sliver of gold appeared at the crest of the farthest hill, heralding the arrival of the morning sun. The sight was glorious, breathtaking in its beauty.

"Do you miss not living here, now that you're governor?" she asked curiously

"Every day."

Hearing the wistfulness in his voice, she hugged his arms to her waist. "Then you should make it a point to come more often," she told him.

He turned his lips against her hair. "Would you come with me?"

She tipped her head back to look up at him and smiled. "Maybe."

Returning her smile, he slid his hands up her middle and covered her breasts. "Just maybe?" He stroked his thumbs across her nipples, making them stiffen and her breath catch in her throat. "That doesn't sound very promising," he murmured. He bent his head over hers. "What if I promise to make the trip worthwhile?" he whispered, before brushing his lips across hers.

Heat crawled from the tips of her toes to curl in ribbons of warmth in her belly. "Mmm," she

hummed silkily, and reached to loop an arm around
his neck. "How?" she asked as she drew his face
closer, the kiss deeper.

He didn't reply, but showed her, shaping his fingers
over her breasts and squeezing as he slipped his
tongue inside her mouth. He teased her with his
hands, his lips, gentle bumps of his nose against hers,
followed by deep thrusts of his tongue, until her body
trembled with need.

She felt the prod of his sex as it grew, lengthening
and hardening against her buttocks, and suddenly
wanted more than anything to have him inside her,
filling her. Twisting around on his lap, she locked her
arms behind his neck as she straddled him, bracing
her knees on the willow chair seat and hugging his
thighs with hers.

"Let me love you," she whispered as she rained
kisses over his face and down his chest. Slowly un-
winding her arms from around his neck, she slid her
hands over his shoulders and down to his abdomen.

He sucked in a breath, tensing, as her fingers en-
circled his sex. She lifted her head to press a soft
smile against his lips. "Let me," she said again and
guided him to her. She swept her tongue across his
teeth as she sank down, taking him in. A groan rose
in his throat and she swallowed the sound, glorying
in the power she felt as she began to slowly ride him.

Pleasure poured through her in waves at the feel of
him moving inside her, and she flowed with it, danced
with it, wanting to share the sensations with him. Everything about him excited her, aroused her: the mus-

cled chest her hands roamed; the short, sleep-mussed hair she ran her fingers through; the taste of him on her tongue; the varying textures of his skin beneath her hands. His sex sliding lazily in and out of her.

Then, suddenly, he dug his fingers into her hips and drew her hard against him, thrusting faster and faster with an urgency that demanded a greater speed, a more desperate race toward satisfaction. The pressure built inside her, ballooning until she was sure she'd explode.

As quickly as he'd increased the pace, he stopped and held her against him. "Wait," he murmured against her lips.

Desperate for the satisfaction that taunted just out of her reach, she tore her mouth from his. "No," she cried, pumping her hips wildly against his in a frantic bid for him to resume the pace.

Instead, he banded his arms around her and pushed to his feet, frustrating her even more. Crazed by the desire that clawed at her, she fought against his arms and pushed at his chest as he guided her legs around his waist.

"No. Please," she sobbed, burying her face in the curve of his neck. She tasted the salt of her own tears, the fever of the passion that heated his skin.

"Shh," he soothed. "Look."

When she stubbornly kept her face tucked in the curve of his neck, he caught her chin and forced her face to the side. She blinked at the haze of passion that clouded her eyes, slowly focusing on the sun as it crowned, spilling an ever widening pool of golden light over the dark hillside. Her eyes widened in awe, and she clung to Gil, entranced by the sight.

On a distant level she felt the nudge of his nose against her jaw, the spread of his smile against her cheek…the slight bow of his body as he pushed inside her. She turned to look at him, her eyes questioning.

With his gaze on hers, he thrust deeper, and pleasure arced through her, forcing the breath from her lungs and his name past her lips on a shocked gasp. He tensed, his eyes darkening, his jaw clenching. She felt his body jerk once…then again and again as he climaxed.

The golden glow of the sunrise seemed to blend with the warmth of his seed and spread slowly to her limbs, setting her body aglow from within. Then, like an explosion, she reached her own climax, the sensation a pulsing stream of light and color that swept through her body, swirling behind her eyes and illuminating her soul. Wanting to hold on to the glorious sensation as long as possible, she arched back, clinging to Gil, her hips melded to his.

Groaning, he began to turn, spinning faster and faster with each revolution, until she was dizzy and laughing. She dropped her head back and flung out her arms, trusting the hands that held her to keep her safe, while she embraced the sunrise, the radiant light that washed over their bodies like a blessing of golds, pinks and lavenders that seemed to come straight from heaven itself.

Four

"**W**ow," Suzy murmured, awed by the spacious kitchen she followed Gil into.

"Like it?"

"Like it," she said incredulously as she turned a slow circle, trying to take it all in. "This is unbelievable!" Running her palm over a counter topped with squares of tumbled stone, she leaned to look out a window that took advantage of the gorgeous view of green pastures and cedar and oak-covered hills in the distance. She glanced his way. "Did you design this yourself?"

He crossed to a beverage center and pulled out the makings for coffee. "Most of it, though I did ask my mother for help with the final layout." He measured grounds into the filter. "I built the house to live in, and since I plan to someday share it with my wife, I figured Mom knew more than I did about what things a woman would want in a kitchen.''

Amazed that he would consider his wife's preferences when he didn't even have one, she could only stare. ''That's really sweet,'' was all she could think of to say.

He shot her a wink. ''No. That's prior planning.'' Chuckling, he switched on the coffeemaker. Then he turned, bracing his hips against the counter and folding his arms across his chest. ''There are those who accuse me of thinking everything to death before I make a decision, my mother included.''

At the second mention of his mother, Suzy couldn't help wondering about their relationship. ''Are you and your mother close?''

He shrugged. ''I suppose. Though no closer than my father and I are. Why do you ask?''

Thinking of the dysfunctional relationship she shared with her own mother, she wandered the kitchen, dragging her hand over the tumbled stone counter and avoiding his gaze. ''No particular reason. Just curious.''

''They live about a mile from here in the old home place. That's where I grew up. What about you? Are you close to your parents?''

She stiffened at the question, then forced her shoulders to relax, pretending interest in the microwave's complicated control panel. ''There's just my mother. My parents divorced when I was young.''

''Your father didn't maintain contact with you?''

She shook her head. "No. But no great loss. From what I remember of him, he was a jerk."

"That's a shame," Gil murmured sympathetically, then smiled. "I'd like for you to meet my parents. I think you'd like them."

And Suzy prayed he'd *never* meet her parents. Especially her father. "Yeah," she replied vaguely. "Whatever." She opened the sack of items they'd purchased at a convenience store on the drive to the ranch the night before. "Hungry?"

Gil watched her pull out the package of sweet rolls, knowing she was trying to change the subject and wondering about it. But he'd let her, he decided. For the time being, anyway. They had the rest of the weekend to get to know each other.

He pushed away from the counter. "Hungrier than a bear." He poured two cups of coffee, then joined her at the breakfast table. Lifting his cup, he blew on his coffee, studying her through the steam that rose above the rim. What a paradox, he thought, suppressing a smile as he let his gaze drift over her freshly scrubbed cheeks, the sleep-mussed blond hair and the delicate curve of one shoulder not quite covered by the shirt he'd loaned her. Or, if not a paradox, she was, at the very least, a talented actress.

From the moment he'd met her, he'd suspected she used the exotic makeup and outrageous clothing as a disguise of sorts to conceal a different personality, a different woman entirely. And when he'd gotten a look at her home, with its cheerful yellow siding, gardens spilling with flowers of every color and description, and the eclectic, yet cozy, collection of furnishings with which she'd filled the interior, he was even more convinced that she wasn't at all like the image she chose to project to the world. All the makeup and clothing was nothing but a facade she hid behind. But from what was she hiding? he asked himself, the question drawing a frown. Or from whom?

She took a bite of her roll, then glanced up, as if sensing his gaze. "What?" she asked, dabbing self-consciously at her mouth.

"Do you realize you've never told me your name?"

If he hadn't been studying her so intently, he would've missed the flash of panic in her eyes before she dropped her gaze and picked up her napkin.

"I told you my name," she said as she wiped the sugary icing from her fingers. "It's Suzy."

"Your *full* name," he persisted.

She looked up and met his gaze squarely, almost defiantly. "Suzy," she repeated, then masked the defiance behind a dazzling smile, meant to disarm him. "I figure if one name is good enough for Madonna and Cher, why not me?"

Though his gut told him to pursue the issue, Gil decided to let it drop, not wanting to chance ruining what remained of their weekend together. He'd already discovered that Suzy was like a young colt unused to human handling, one who spooked easily and unexpectedly. One who required a gentle and patient hand. "So you plan to pursue an acting and musical career?"

At his teasing, she cocked a saucy brow. "Maybe. Think I could?"

Chuckling, he shook his head. "I don't know. Do you sing?"

"In the shower."

He lifted his cup in a salute. "That's a start." He took a sip, winking at her over the cup's rim. "But you could probably get by on your beauty alone."

She rolled her eyes. "Yeah, I'm sure I look really beautiful right now without a smidgen of makeup on and wearing one of your old shirts."

He set down his cup and selected a sweet roll. "You don't need makeup. In fact, you're even more beautiful without it." He took a bite of the pastry, his eyes filling with amusement. "And as far as the shirt goes, the only way you could possibly look better is without it."

"You politicians," she said, dismissing the compliment with a flap of her hand. "You're full of nothing but a lot of hot air."

He leveled a finger at her nose. "I've already told you once. I'm no politician. And I don't lie, either. When I tell you something, you can bank on it being the truth."

Relieved that the conversation had taken a different direction, Suzy folded her hands beneath her chin. "Okay," she said, accepting his warning as a challenge. "If you speak only the truth, then tell me what it is about me that you find so attractive?"

Hooking his thumbs in the waist of his jeans, he

rocked his chair back on two legs. "Where do you want me to start?"

"The list is that long?"

"Long enough." Chuckling, he dropped his chair back down and leaned to rest his forearms on the table. "But I'll give you the *Reader's Digest* condensed version. From the first, you intrigued me. Most people, once they find out I'm the governor, treat me differently. Like I'm somebody special or something. You don't and didn't from the beginning. In fact, you were downright rude."

"I wasn't rude! I was busy and you were in my way."

"You were rude."

"Okay," she said, conceding the point only because she was anxious to hear more. "So I was rude."

"And that's what intrigued me. Most folks would've stopped what they were doing and tripped all over themselves in an effort to please me or impress me. But not you." He laughed and shook his head. "I liked that."

"You were attracted to me because I was rude," she summarized sourly. "That's certainly gratifying."

"That was only the first thing that attracted me." He picked up his cup and took a sip. "Then there was the sex."

She held up a hand. "Uh-uh. There wasn't any sex. At least not initially."

"No, but the idea was there. The question of

whether or not it would be good between us. You were wondering about it, too."

"I certainly was not!"

He reached across the table and caught her chin in his hand. "You were, too. At the party you catered, and again the afternoon I came to your house. Come on," he prodded, stroking a thumb persuasively across her lower lip. "Admit it."

Scowling, she pushed his hand away. "Okay," she said grudgingly. "So maybe I was. But only briefly," she added stubbornly. "I assure you I didn't lose any sleep over whether or not we would be sexually compatible."

"I did."

Surprised that he would confess his infatuation with her so freely, she was tempted to ask him to elaborate, but feared if she did he'd expect the same of her in turn. "Why haven't you ever married?" she asked instead.

"Never found the right woman."

"In thirty-six years you've never met *one* woman you would consider marrying?"

His eyes twinkled mischievously. "Nope."

She pressed her lips together and eyed him dubiously. "It's rumored that you haven't married because you're gay."

He lifted a brow. "Do you think I'm gay?"

She choked on a laugh. "Hardly. But doesn't it bother you that they print lies about you?"

"Why should it? *I* know it's not true."

"Yeah, but don't you think some people accept what they read as the gospel?"

"I suppose they might."

"And that doesn't bother you?" she asked in disbelief.

"No. Should it?"

"Well, yes!" she cried and pushed to her feet. "The media shouldn't be allowed to print lies about you or anybody else for that matter." She marched to the sink and dumped out her coffee. "It's an invasion of a person's privacy, a direct infringement of an individual's personal right to life, liberty and the pursuit of happiness, as guaranteed by the constitution of the United States."

Surprised by her fervor, Gil rose, too, and followed her to the sink. He stuck his cup under the faucet, glancing her way as he rinsed it out. "The constitution also promises freedom of speech and press."

"To speak and print lies?" she returned. "I think not." She turned and paced away. "The media should report only the truth and leave it at that. They shouldn't be allowed to sensationalize the news just to increase their readership and up their ratings."

"No, they shouldn't," he agreed. "So how do you think we should go about putting a stop to it?"

Suzy whirled. "We? As in you and me?"

"Yeah. Obviously you feel strongly about this topic. Why not take your anger and put it to good use?"

She took a step in retreat, horrified at the thought of placing herself in direct contact—and possibly conflict—with the media. "I...I couldn't. I don't know anything about the law or politics."

"You don't have to. All you have to have is a desire to change things and the courage to take a stand for what you believe is right."

She took another step back, shaking her head. "I couldn't," she said again. "I wouldn't know the first thing about how to begin. I'm a caterer, not a politician."

"And I'm a rancher," he reminded her pointedly, then softened the scolding with a smile. "You've already taken the first step, whether you realize it or not. You've recognized a wrong that needs to be righted."

Fearing that if she didn't do something and quickly, he would appoint her chairman of a committee to investigate media practices or something equally frightening, Suzy did what she always did when she found herself in an uncomfortable situation. She fell back on sarcasm. "Yeah," she scoffed, "and after I whip the media back into shape, I think I'll start on health care reform. Now that's a topic that really stirs my blood."

"There's need for change there, as well, both on a state and national level."

"Yeah. Whatever." She faked a yawn and stretched lazily. "All this talk about changing the world is making me tired," she said wearily. "Want to take a nap?"

He shook his head. "As tempting as I find that

proposition, I need to check on my cattle. You can ride along with me, if you like.''

"On horses?"

"Horseback is the only way to reach some of the land we'd be traveling."

She shuddered. "If it's all the same to you, I think I'll stay right here and nap. I didn't get very much sleep last night," she reminded him drolly.

Gil collected his cowboy hat from the counter and settled it over his head as he opened the back door. "And if I have anything to say about it, you won't be getting any tonight, either."

Suzy did try to nap, but sleep evaded her; her mind churned with memories and fears stirred by her conversation with Gil about the media. Every time she closed her eyes, she saw the headlines that screamed her father's misdeeds to the world, heard the incessant ringing of the phone and the heartbreaking sound of her mother's hysterical sobbing. But most of all, she saw *him*. Her father. The infamous Reverend Bobby Swain. With his perfectly coifed hair, his custom-made suit, standing with his arms uplifted, eyes closed, wearing a beatific smile…the same smile he had used to win unsuspecting women into his fold and eventually into his bed.

And the media had reported it all.

When the rumor of his misdeeds had first surfaced, like hounds on a hunt, reporters had chased and dug until they'd uncovered all the reverend's dark secrets and exposed him for the fornicator he was. But in their glee of tearing down the temple of sin the reverend had created for himself, they'd destroyed Suzy's mother, as well. When the first story had broken, Suzy remembered watching her mother on television, the beautiful and regal Sarah Swain, standing stoically at her husband's side, her loyal and loving gaze fixed on him as he denied the stories printed about him, contending that they were the work of the devil in an effort to destroy his ministry.

But with each new woman the media dragged before the camera with her claim that she, too, had had an affair with the famous TV evangelist, Sarah Swain's faith in her husband, as well as her emotional stability, had slowly dwindled away, until she was merely a shadow of the confident and loving mother Suzy had once known.

The media had destroyed their entire family structure, dragged her mother's name onto the front page right along with the reverend's, heaping shame and humiliation upon the family, until Sarah had finally collapsed beneath it. At Sarah's parents' insistence and under their direction, she had divorced Bobby Swain, changed her name and secretly relocated in Elgin, a small rural town east of Austin, Texas, in hopes of protecting herself and her daughter from any further humiliation.

Though the scandal had destroyed their family, it hadn't harmed Bobby Swain…at least, not for long. He'd weathered the storm seemingly unscathed and continued to preach his message from the pulpit, gathering more and more followers, while lining his pockets with their donations. But all that had ended when a disgruntled contributor had sued the reverend for misappropriation of church funds. The lawsuit that followed was what had finally destroyed him, and he wound up locked behind a set of gates that were anything but pearly.

During that second scandal Suzy realized that her mother's attempt to escape her association and relation to the reverend by changing her name and moving were in vain. The media had scoured court records until they had tracked down Sarah and Suzy in Elgin. They began to print allegations that the reverend had secretly funneled funds to his former wife and daughter that rightfully belonged to the church. Mother and daughter took another beating by the press that lasted for months after the reverend was locked away in prison.

It was then that Suzy had decided to quit using her last name entirely and had pumped up her efforts to look and act nothing like a preacher's daughter.

She had good reason to hate and avoid the media, she reminded herself. And that's why she didn't want to go head-to-head in a battle with them, as Gil had suggested. For her mother's sake, as much as her own, she wanted, *needed* to maintain her privacy, guard her identity, keep her relationship to the reverend in the past where it belonged.

But how she could do that and continue to see Gil?

With a groan, she rolled from the bed and scraped back her hair, digging her palms against her temples. She couldn't possibly have a relationship with Gil without the media finding out and dragging out all her family's dirty laundry to air again. And her mother would never survive another battering by the press. Her health and her emotional stability were much too fragile for her to suffer through all that again.

Suzy dropped her arms and forced herself to calm down, telling herself she was only borrowing trouble. So far no one knew that she was seeing Gil. And after this weekend there would be nothing to know. When they returned to Austin, they'd go their separate ways, Gil to the governor's mansion and she to her home, and it would be over.

Oddly she found that reassurance more depressing than comforting.

Knowing she needed to focus her mind on something else, she wandered to the kitchen and dug around until she'd found enough ingredients to throw together a meal, taking solace in the familiar activity of cooking. As she worked, she rid herself of the melancholy that stubbornly lingered by experimenting with all the fancy gadgets and state-of-the-art equipment Gil's mother had selected for her son's future wife.

It was while stooping to check on the roast she'd placed in the oven that she recalled Gil's earlier comment. *A wife to share my home with someday,* she remembered him saying.

A yearning spread through her as his words echoed in her mind, and she moved to stand before the window above the sink, hugging her arms around her waist as she stared outside. Even though she knew it was impossible—stupid even to entertain such fanciful thoughts when she knew their relationship would have to end with the weekend—she couldn't help wishing that she could be the woman with whom Gil would someday share his home.

As she stared, her mind clouded with if-only dreams, Gil rode into her line of vision and dragged her from her thoughts. She leaned closer to the window, watching as he loped his horse toward the corral. He looked so natural in the saddle, so at ease, so...masculine. And when he reined the horse to a stop and swung down from the saddle, she pressed her hand against her heart, experiencing for the first time that ''pitter-patter'' she remembered him claiming he felt each time he thought about her.

Could she be falling in love with him? she asked herself, her blood chilling at the mere thought.

Lust, she reminded herself and turned from the window and ran outside, suddenly impatient to see him, to touch him.

''Gil!'' she shouted, waving her hand over her head as she ran toward the corral.

In the act of slipping the bridle from the horse's head, he glanced up, and a smile slowly spread across his face. He hooked the bridle over a post, closed the corral gate behind him, then turned and opened his arms. Suzy ran into them, laughing when he scooped her off her feet and up against his chest.

Pressing back in his arms, she looked down at him,

her laughter giving way to a lusty sigh. Unable to resist, she plucked off his hat, tossed it aside, then planted a kiss full on his mouth.

"Hey," he said. "What's this all about?"

Her gaze on his, she combed her fingers through the damp crease his hat had left on his hair. "I missed you."

"Damn," he murmured, grinning. "Maybe I ought to leave you alone more often."

She fixed a mean look on her face. "Try it, cowboy," she warned, "and you might find yourself tied to my bed."

"Mmm-mmm." He hitched her higher on his chest. "This is sounding better and better all the time."

Laughing, she dropped a kiss on his mouth. "Hungry?"

"For you? Always."

She pushed at his shoulders to put her down. "I was talking about food."

He deposited her on her feet. "You cooked something for us to eat?"

"No," she replied dryly. "I ordered takeout."

Draping an arm along her shoulders, he headed her toward the house. "I hope it's Chinese. I've had a yearning for chow-mein all day."

"Very funny."

He bumped his hip playfully against hers. "You started it. So what did you cook?"

"Beef with a mushroom cream sauce, green beans and roasted onions. It was all I could find to make a meal." She slanted him a disapproving look. "Your pantry is pitifully bare."

He shrugged. "I'm not here often enough to warrant stocking in a large supply of groceries."

With her gaze going to the wide expanse of green pastures and the hills in the distance, she slipped an arm around his waist. "I don't know how you manage to stay away," she said with a sigh. "If this was my home—"

Gil jerked to a stop, pulling Suzy to a stop, as well.

"What?" she asked, glancing up at him, then turned her head to follow his gaze.

"Somebody's coming."

He'd no sooner voiced the warning, than she saw a car top the ridge. She dropped her arm from his waist and stepped away, putting distance between them. "Who is it?"

He squinted his eyes, trying to identify the vehicle, then swore. "Skinner."

Suzy whipped her head around to stare at Gil, her eyes wide with alarm. "Paul Skinner? The reporter?"

Frowning, Gil braced his hands on his hips. "Yeah."

Suzy spun for the house, but Gil caught her arm, stopping her. "Too late now," he said with a jerk of his chin toward the rapidly approaching car. "He's already spotted us."

Eyes blazing, she wrenched free and ran.

Gil started after her, then stopped and, with a frustrated sigh, turned back to wait for the reporter.

Skinner braked to a stop and climbed out, lifting a hand in greeting. "Afternoon, Governor."

"Paul," Gil replied, acknowledging the greeting, but not returning the man's smile. "What brings you out this way?"

"Dropped by the mansion earlier today and was told you were out of town for the weekend. Put two and two together and figured you were here at your ranch."

"This is usually where I come when I want to get away for some downtime. I make no secret of that."

Gil's subtle reminder that Paul was invading his private time went right over the reporter's head. Or at least the man pretended it did as he stuck his hands in his pockets and rocked back on his heels, looking around. "Nice place you've got here," he commented.

Gil set his jaw, struggling to remain civil, knowing nothing would be gained by antagonizing the reporter. "I think so. Was there something specific you needed?" he asked, hoping to hurry the reporter on his way.

"Nope. Just wanted to get a gander at where the governor of Texas spends his free time. I'm thinking about doing a series of articles along that line." Paul's gaze reached the house and lingered there a moment, then he glanced at Gil, a brow arched expectantly. "Seems I scared off your guest. I hope I didn't interrupt anything."

Knowing that the reporter had indeed spotted Suzy and was fishing for an explanation of her hasty departure, Gil shook his head. "No. Not at all." He slung a companionable arm along the man's shoulder and turned him around, strolling along with him as he headed him back to his car. "That article you mentioned sounds mighty interesting. I'll have to plan a barbecue and invite all the media out for a tour of the ranch."

They reached the car and Gil leaned around Paul to open the door and added with a wink, "I'll personally see that you receive an invitation." He waited until Paul climbed inside, then slammed the door behind him and stuck his head in the window. "By the way, Paul," he said, "a closed gate around these parts means the same as a locked door to you city boys. Pass through one uninvited, and you're liable to find your butt shot full of lead."

Scowling, Paul reached for the key. "Yeah. I'll remember that."

Gil straightened and slapped a hand against the top of the car. "Mind that you do." He took a step back. "Watch out for armadillos on the drive back to town. Those dang critters think roads were built for their personal crossing."

Paul jerked the gearshift down. "Yeah, I will," he muttered.

Gil watched the reporter wheel his car around and head back the way he'd come. When the car topped the ridge and disappeared on the other side, he turned for the house.

When he entered the kitchen, he found Suzy standing at the sink, her arms buried to the elbows in dishwater. He could tell by the stiffness in her shoulders, in the jerkiness of her movements that the reporter's visit had upset her.

Hoping to reassure her, he crossed to stand behind her and slipped his arms around her waist. "No need to fret. He's gone now."

She whirled, and he was stunned to see that her face was flushed with anger and her eyes gleamed with tears. "You promised," she accused and twisted from his embrace. She stalked away, then swung back, dragging a hand beneath her nose. "You said that the media would never know we were here. Trust me, you said!" She tossed up her hands, sending soap bubbles flying. "And fool that I am, I did!"

"Suzy—"

When he started toward her, she pushed out a hand. "No. Don't. I don't want you to touch me. Not ever again. I just want to go home."

Gil stopped, reining in his own anger, his need to hold her, knowing that any movement at all from him would only upset her more. Like a colt when cornered, she would kick and fight against anything or anyone who drew too close. So he waited, watching until the rapid rise and fall of her breasts slowed, the trembling in her hands stilled. He waited until she sank to the floor in a heap and buried her face in her hands, sobbing.

Then he went to her. He eased down on the floor beside her and gathered her into his arms. She turned into his chest willingly and buried her face against his neck, clinging to him with a desperation that closed his throat and made any attempt to comfort her with words impossible.

So he soothed her with his hands, with his lips, with whispered murmurs that had no meaning, made no sense, just comforting sounds that vibrated against her hair, her cheeks, her lips. He held her until the sobs stopped, until the trembling in her body ceased. Then he held her tighter, holding her close to his chest, to his heart.

"I'm sorry, Suzy," he murmured, pressing his lips against her hair. "I'm so, so sorry."

She inhaled a shuddery breath and slowly eased from his embrace, dragging her hands beneath her eyes. "No. I am. It wasn't your fault. I shouldn't have blamed you. I was just so...so mad."

He tucked a knuckle beneath her chin and tipped her face up to his. "You forgive me, then?"

She smiled a watery smile, unable to do any less than he asked. Laying a palm along his cheek, she said, "Yes, I forgive you. But I still want to go home. I should never have come here in the first place."

He covered her hand with his. "Why, Suzy? Tell me why?"

She stared into his eyes, seeing the confusion that swirled in the blue depths, the need for understanding. She wanted to tell him everything. Bare her soul and put an end to the charade. Expose the identity she'd struggled for years to hide. The words were there on the tip of her tongue, in her heart. But she couldn't voice them. Not when she stood to lose so much. The loss of her privacy. The loss of the identity she'd worked so hard to assume.

But as she continued to meet his gaze, held by the warmth that had first drawn her to him, the comfort and tenderness that she knew lay beneath, she realized her biggest fear was Gil's reaction. That was what kept her silent, the words locked inside. Would he be shocked if she were to tell him who her father was? Would disgust and revulsion replace the confusion that now swirled in his eyes? Would he turn away from her in loathing? Would he take her home as she'd requested and never want to see her again? Worse, would his association with her ruin his effectiveness as governor? Taint the record of a man who wanted only to serve?

He'd given her nothing but honesty from the first, she told herself, feeling the tears choke her. And what had she given him in return? Nothing but artful evasion and glib replies to all his questions. Knowing he deserved so much more, more than she'd ever given any man, she slowly drew her hand from beneath his.

"All right," she said, then firmed her lips to control their trembling. "But it's not pretty," she warned.

He caught her hand in his and squeezed. "What we fear usually isn't. But sometimes when we hoard our fears, keep them to ourselves, they seem bigger, more insurmountable than they really are."

She would've laughed at that if she weren't so choked by tears at his kindness, at his offer of understanding. Unable to meet his gaze any longer, she dropped her chin and rubbed her thumb across his knuckles, searching for the courage she needed to share her secrets. "It's my father," she began hesitantly. She lifted her gaze, needing to see his reaction when she told him. "My father is Reverend Bobby Swain."

A frown furrowed his brow, as if the name meant nothing to him, then slowly smoothed as recognition dawned.

"Bobby Swain?" he repeated, as if unsure he'd heard her correctly.

She nodded, shame heating her cheeks. "Y-yes." She watched his face, waiting for the revulsion to come, knowing she had to tell him all. "I haven't seen him since I was six years old. Mother changed our names and moved us to Elgin after she divorced him."

Though his gaze remained on hers, his expression free of any emotion, she sensed the shock her announcement drew.

Sighing, she eased her hand from his and started to rise. "So now you know why I hate the media, why it's impossible for me to see you again."

He caught her hand and tugged her back down to his lap. "No, I don't." When she tried to stand, he vised his arms around her waist, forcing her to remain on his lap. "I know only that your father was a less-than-honorable man and that you don't want to be associated with him."

She shoved at his chest. "Don't you understand?" she cried. "If the media finds out who I am, it'll start all over again. They'll dig out all the old stories and print them again.''

''You have nothing to be ashamed of. You did nothing wrong.''

''But he did!'' she screamed. ''And I'm his daughter!''

When he remained silent, his gaze steady and unflinching on hers, Suzy groaned, fisting her hands against his chest. ''Think, Gil. Think how having your name associated with mine will affect your popularity with the public, your hopes of accomplishing anything during your term as governor.''

''And it may have no effect whatsoever.''

She pushed against his arms, managing this time to break free and rise. ''Are you nuts?'' she shouted down at him. ''Of course it will have an effect! They'll drag your name through the dirt right along with mine, and you'll lose all your credibility, all your support.''

He pushed to his feet, never once moving his gaze from hers. ''I'm willing to take that chance.''

''Well, I'm not! And I won't let you!''

He caught her by her elbows and drew her to him, a smile curving the corners of his mouth. ''I love a woman with gumption.''

She flattened her hands against his chest, desperate to make him understand. ''Gil, please. Listen to me. You don't know what you're saying, what all you stand to lose. I've been there. I've seen what the press can do to a person. I—''

He closed his mouth over hers, silencing her warnings. She struggled against him, trying to twist free, but he only tightened his arms around her. Tears stung her eyes at his stubbornness…and the tenderness with which he kissed her.

Unfurling her fingers from the fists she'd curled against his chest, she lifted her hands and wrapped them around his neck. She felt his smile against her lips, the increased pressure on her mouth when he stooped to catch her beneath the knees. Knowing it was useless to fight him, she let him carry her to his room and to his bed, determined to make him listen once he released her.

But when he laid her down, then stood looking at her, his eyes filled with a desire that set her skin on fire, all argument melted from her tongue. And when he ripped open her shirt—his shirt—and dropped down to capture the budded peak of a breast between his teeth, her mind went blank. She could only think of the cleverness of the mouth that suckled her, the heat that raced through her veins, the arrows of sensation his suckling shot to her belly.

And having him inside her.

Five

"Suzy?"

Sprawled across Gil, she could only manage a weak, "Hmm."

"I don't think this is just lust."

She flipped her eyes wide, but in the darkness she couldn't see his expression, only his shadowed profile. "You don't?"

"Uh-uh." He rolled to his side and gathered her into his arms. He bumped his nose against hers, the stretch of his smile spreading along her jaw. "I don't think I'll ever get enough of you."

She tensed, the fears he'd distracted her from by carrying her off to bed returning with a vengeance. "Gil…"

"What?"

She sat up, scraping her hair back and holding it away from her face, trying to find the right words to convince him that this was a mistake. She quickly discovered there weren't any. "We can't do this."

He pushed himself to an elbow. "I know it'll be tough. But we can find a way to keep the media out of our relationship."

She bolted from the bed. "I'd think that Paul Skinner's appearance today would have proved to you how impossible that is."

His eyebrows drew together as he watched her snatch up his shirt and push her arms into the sleeves. "No. It just proved to me that I need to take better advantage of all the security that's provided for me."

She stopped with her back to him and squeezed her eyes shut, knowing that all the security in the world wasn't enough to keep out the press. Not when they smelled a story.

Slowly she turned to face him. "Gil," she said carefully. "It would never work. You know that. When your term is over—"

He rocketed from the bed and to his feet. "When my term is over?" he repeated. "Hell, that's *three* years from now!"

"I know it is. But that's the best option I have to offer."

"Well, it's not good enough." His anger faded as quickly as it had appeared. He crossed to her and caught her hands, squeezing them within his own. "Suzy, I don't want this to end here. I *won't* let it end here."

Tears threatened at the desperation she saw in his eyes. "It has to."

He gripped her hands tighter. "Dammit, it doesn't!"

"We can't see each other as long as you're governor."

He dropped her hands and turned away, rubbing at the sudden tension in his neck. "I won't walk away from my duties as governor. I can't."

Tears flooded her eyes that he'd even consider that as an option. "I'd never ask you to."

He swung back around to face her. "Then give me a chance. *Us* a chance. There's a way we can pull this off. I know there is. There are things I can do to protect you from the press. I can—"

She dropped her chin to her chest and shook her head. "You couldn't. You saw the proof of that as well as I did today."

He grabbed her by the arms. "I won't give you up. And I sure as hell won't wait until my term is over to see you again."

"Gil—"

"No," he said fiercely. Then, groaning, he dragged her against his chest and crushed her to him. "We can make this work, Suzy." Rocking her back and forth, he pressed his lips against her hair. "I know we can."

She knew better than to believe him. She'd already seen how easily the press could scale the walls of his privacy, invade what should rightfully be his private life. But she desperately wanted what he wanted.

Time together. The chance to play this out. The opportunity for a normal life. A life that perhaps included him.

Lifting her face, she met his gaze and did what she'd sworn she would never do again. She placed her trust in a man. This man. And she did so for the second time.

Surprisingly cheerful for such an ungodly hour and after such an emotionally draining weekend with so little sleep, Suzy kneaded dough while swaying her hips to the beat of the Platters' song currently playing on the oldies station she had tuned her radio to.

In spite of her apprehensions and arguments to the contrary, Gil had finally convinced her to see him on the sly until he could come up with a way to make his involvement with her public without harming either of them. Though she found the whole idea of sneaking around distasteful, the idea of waiting three years to be with him was even more so. But as Gil had said, if they were careful—

A knock sounded at her back door and she glanced at the oven clock in surprise, wondering who would be dropping by this early in the morning.

Wiping her hands across the front of her apron, she crossed to the back door and opened it. A smile of delight spread across her face when she saw that it was Penny on her stoop. "Hey, girlfriend. What are you doing out so early?"

Pushing past her, Penny stormed into the kitchen.

"Where have you been all weekend? I've called you a thousand times."

Surprised by her friend's anger, Suzy closed the door. "Sorry. I was out of town."

Penny flopped down on a chair at the table and snatched her purse to her lap. "You might've called and told me."

Hearing the tears in her friend's voice, Suzy started across the room. "What is it?" she asked in concern. "Has something happened to Erik? Have you left him?"

Penny sniffled, waving away Suzy's fears. "No. He's fine. We're fine." Her eyes full of tears, she caught Suzy's hand and pulled her down onto the chair next to hers. "Have you seen the Sunday paper?"

Dread hit Suzy like a bucket of cold water on the face. "No. Why?"

Penny let go of her hand to pull a newspaper from her purse. "Prepare yourself," she warned, dabbing at her eyes as she offered the folded paper to Suzy. "It's in Paul Skinner's column."

Suzy tore her gaze from Penny's to stare at the newspaper, then unfolded it and began to read. She'd read only three lines before she leaped to her feet. "It was a private party," she cried, wadding the paper in her fist. "The press wasn't even invited. How did he get in?"

"I doubt he did."

Suzy spun, holding the fisted paper above her head. "Then how do you explain *this?*" She dropped her arm and snapped open the paper, her voice filled with bitterness as she read, "'More than a few guests were shocked at Friday night's gala celebrating the opening of the hospital's new wing, when a young woman, decked out in an outfit better suited for one of the girls at LaGrange's infamous Chicken Ranch, attempted to crash the party, insisting she was the governor's date. Guests were even more shocked when the governor acknowledged the woman's claim by offering her his arm and remaining by her side throughout the evening's festivities.'"

Suzy slapped the paper against her leg, her face flushed with rage. "Now you tell me how Paul Skinner could possibly know what I was wearing if he wasn't there?"

"You know as well as I do that gossip columnists have sources who provide them with information. Someone probably saw you at the party and called him, anxious to be the first to share the juicy tidbit."

Suzy's lip curled in a snarl. "The slimeball."

Sniffing, Penny gestured at the paper. "What about that part at the end? The part where he mentions seeing a woman with the governor at his ranch. Was that where you were all weekend?"

Not having read that far, Suzy paled. Her fingers trembling, she opened the paper and scanned to the paragraph Penny had mentioned. "'Since the governor was seen in the company of at least one, perhaps two women this weekend,'" she read aloud, "'one can only assume that the previous rumors concerning his sexual preferences were nothing but malicious mudslinging, planted by those opposed to his unorthodox manner of conducting government business. Oh, and by the way, Governor, was that one of your shirts the young woman seen with you at your ranch was wearing?' ''

Ripping the paper in two, she flung the pieces away from her. ''That slimeball!'' she cried. ''That vicious, sneaky slimeball!''

Penny caught her lower lip between her teeth and rose. ''He didn't mention you by name. Maybe he doesn't know who you are.''

Suzy slammed her fists to her hips. ''And how long do you think it will take him to track down the mysterious woman the governor escorted around the dedication, considering Gil introduced me as Suzy to nearly everyone there?'' Knowing only too well the answer, she buried her face in her hands. ''Oh, I knew this would happen,'' she wailed. ''I just knew it!''

The telephone rang and she snatched her hands down to stare at it in horror.

Penny took a hesitant step forward. ''Do you want me to answer it?''

Suzy flung out an arm to stop her. ''No...I will.'' She drew in a deep breath, then picked up the receiver. ''Hello?'' She listened a moment, then banged down the receiver.

''Who was it?'' Penny asked as Suzy stormed past her to the island. ''A reporter?''

Suzy snatched up her rolling pin. ''No. The governor.''

"And you hung up on him?" Penny asked in dismay.

Suzy whacked the rolling pin against the last remaining mound of dough and began to roll it furiously back and forth. "You dang right I did. I don't need this nightmare." She dashed a hand beneath her nose, angered even more by the tears. "I should've just told him to go to hell in the first place and been done with it."

"Oh, Suzy," Penny murmured, crossing to place a comforting hand on her friend's shoulder. "You can't hide from the world forever."

Suzy stopped rolling and turned to fix Penny with a steely-eyed look. "Wanna bet?"

"Get me some backing on the drought aid for farmers in West Texas and we'll talk." Gil glanced up as his secretary slipped into his office and quickly covered the phone's mouthpiece with his hand. "Were you able to reach her?"

She shook her head. "Sorry. Still no answer."

Pressing his lips together, Gil moved his hand from the mouthpiece. "Fine," he snapped into the receiver. "We'll talk then." He dropped the phone back onto its base, then slumped back in his chair and turned his head to stare out the window on his left, wishing he could get his hands on Paul Skinner's scrawny neck. What he'd give for five minutes alone in a dark alley with the bastard.

"Governor?" his secretary said hesitantly. "If

there's nothing else pressing, the lieutenant governor is waiting to see you. He said it's important.''

Sighing, Gil sat up and pulled his chair back up to his desk. ''Tell him to come on in.''

He pulled out his itinerary for the day, looking for a break in his schedule that would allow him the time to drop by Suzy's house. She was there, he told himself. She was simply hiding from the press...and obviously from him.

A newspaper landed on his desk, and he glanced up, frowning at Richard Marvin, his lieutenant governor, the man who had tossed it there. ''I see you've seen the paper, too.''

Richard dropped down on the chair opposite the desk and reared back, rolling the ever-present toothpick to the corner of his mouth. ''Yeah, I saw it. The question is, is it true?''

''Which part? That the dress she wore to the dedication was better suited for one of the girls at the Chicken Ranch in LaGrange? Or that she was wearing one of my shirts at my ranch?''

Sighing, Richard pulled the toothpick from his mouth. ''I take it both are true.''

Gil leaned back in his chair, folding his hands behind his head. ''Essentially. Though I would argue Skinner's description of the outfit she wore to the dedication. I've seen teenage girls at the mall dressed in getups a lot more risqué than what Suzy had on.''

Richard scowled. ''This is serious, Gil.''

Gil dropped his arms. ''I know it is.''

"I guess my next question, then, should be what are you going to do about it?"

"Nothing."

"Nothing?" Richard repeated, rising. "Do you realize the damage this kind of piece can do to your credibility? Your ability to successfully push through the legislation you've campaigned so hard for?"

Hearing his lieutenant governor repeat almost the same warnings Suzy had voiced drew a wan smile from Gil. "Yeah. I'm aware."

"And you're going to take this lying down?"

"I didn't say that."

"No, but you *did* say that you weren't going to do anything about it. What you *should* do is request a retraction, hold a news conference and offer some kind of explanation, denying your involvement with this woman."

"I won't do that. It would be a lie."

Richard dropped down to the chair and let his head fall back. "Please tell me she can be bought. That we can pay her off to keep her quiet."

"I'd never do that."

Richard lowered his chin to glower at Gil. "You don't have to. *I'll* see that it's done."

Gil rose and crossed to the window that faced the capitol in the distance, needing the reminder of his responsibilities, the reasons he had sought this office in the first place. He knew things like this went on. From the beginning of time, public figures had erred, sinned, then made deals behind closed doors and passed money under tables to keep their misdeeds from becoming public knowledge.

But the men who had done those things weren't Gil Riley. In his opinion their way was the cowardly way. And Gil Riley was no coward. And, in his mind at least, he hadn't committed any sins. Not when the woman he was involved with was the first one he had ever seriously considered spending the rest of his life with.

"No," he said and turned to face Richard. "I won't let you do that. I'm entitled to a life separate from this office. And what I do on my own time should have no effect on my work here."

Richard snorted. "You're kidding, right?"

"No. I'm dead serious."

Richard pushed slowly to his feet. "Listen, Gil. You aren't John Wayne and this isn't some movie you're starring in, so don't think the audience is going to stand up and cheer because you defended a woman's virtue. This is the real world. People fight dirty here. Things don't operate the way you think they do."

"Maybe not. But they should. I never claimed to be perfect, Richard. No man is. To pretend otherwise would just be building on a lie that's existed too damn long."

"And there's nothing I can do to change your mind?"

"Not on this."

Clamping the toothpick between his teeth again, Richard shook his head as he headed for the door.

"God be with you, then, son, because the press is going to rip your guts out and feed it to the public and laugh like banshees while they're doing it."

Over a week had passed since the weekend Gil had spent with Suzy at his ranch...and the ugly article had appeared in the paper. But a previously scheduled trip to Washington to meet with other state governors had prevented him from attempting any further contact with Suzy. But now the time for a showdown had come.

He knew he was taking a chance on making a fool of himself and possibly making an already bad situation worse, but he was willing to take the gamble, if it meant seeing her again and talking to her.

Dressed all in black and feeling like a cat burglar, he parked two blocks from her house and crept through the dark neighborhood, keeping to the shadows. When he reached her house, he darted across the lawn and through the gate that opened to her backyard. Breathing a sigh of relief that he'd made it that far without detection, he tipped his head back and looked up at the dark windows, trying to decide which marked her bedroom.

With only three to choose from, he picked up a rock and threw it against the glass closest to him. It hit with a *thunk,* then rolled back down the roof and to the ground. He waited, praying that he'd chosen the right one and Suzy would appear at the window. When a minute or more passed without a sign of her, he picked up another rock and threw it at the second window.

Another *thunk*, the rattle of stone striking against the shingles as the rock rolled down the roof sounding like a symphony of bass drums in the silence. A dog barked somewhere down the street, and Gil grabbed another rock, desperate to rouse Suzy before the dog woke the whole neighborhood.

Just as he wound up for another throw, a light went on in the room, and a shadow appeared behind the sheer drapes.

"Suzy?" he called, trying to keep his voice as low as possible, yet be heard.

Snatching back the drapes, she shoved up the window and stuck her head outside. "What are you doing here?" she whispered angrily. "Go away!" She ducked back inside and started to lower the window.

"Suzy!" he shouted. "Please," he begged. "We need to talk."

She pushed her head out the window. "No! Now get out of here before someone sees you."

A light went on in the house next door. Gladys Kravitz's house, Gil remembered...and began to smile. He waited a moment, listening, and choked back a laugh when he heard Suzy's phone ring.

Spying a tree growing close to the corner of the house, he jogged over to it, grabbed a limb and swung himself up. He climbed higher, until he found a limb that fanned out over the second story, then tightrope walked along it, leaping onto the roof when the branch began to bend beneath his weight.

He made his way carefully to the window and lifted it, relieved when he found she hadn't taken the time to lock it. Sitting down on the sill, he threw first one leg over, then the other.

She whirled to glare at him as he dropped down into her room, the phone pressed to her ear. "No, Mrs. Woodley," she said into the receiver. "You don't need to call the police. I'm fine. And I don't see anything out of the ordinary in my backyard."

She rolled her eyes. "Yes, I'm sure. In fact I'm looking out my window right now. It was probably that old tomcat of Mrs. Pruett's on the prowl." She pursed her lips, listening. "Yes, ma'am, I know her cat does his business in the flower pots on your porch. And yes, I really do think that Mrs. Pruett should be forced to control her pets."

Sending up a silent thanks for nosy neighbors, Gil crossed to Suzy and lifted her hair from her neck to nibble there.

She swatted at his head. "Listen, Mrs. Woodley," she said, her breath growing short as he skimmed his lips lower, "I'm going back to bed now. Why don't you do the same? Thanks for calling."

Gil took the receiver from her hand and replaced it on the base.

"Are you crazy?" she whispered angrily. "She might have called the police instead of me!"

Shifting in front of her, Gil slipped his hands beneath her hair, lifted it off her shoulders, then dropped it behind her back. "But she didn't." He bent his head to nibble on her neck again.

"She was going to," Suzy insisted, struggling to escape the pleasure of the feel of his lips against her skin. But she quickly discovered that he'd managed to trap her between himself and the bed and there was no escape left to her. "Gil! Stop it!"

He slid his hands down her arms and linked his hands behind her waist. Rubbing his groin against her middle, he smiled down at her. "Why? Mrs. Kravitz has gone back to bed. I heard you tell her to go there myself."

She pressed her hands against his chest and leaned back as far as she could, desperate to put distance between them. "Her name isn't Kravitz. It's Woodley."

"Okay. Then, Mrs. Woodley has gone back to bed." He bent his knees to peer out the window. "Yep," he said, smiling smugly as he straightened. "Her light's already out. We're all alone."

"We're *not* alone. And as long as you're governor, we'll *never* be alone." She gave his chest an angry shove. "Now get out of here."

Her push didn't budge him, but it did manage to wipe the smile off his face. Narrowing his eyes, he forced a knee between her thighs. "I'm not going anywhere until we talk this through."

Before he'd voiced the warning completely, Suzy found herself flat on her back on her bed and him stretched along her length, his face only inches from her own. "Now," he said, obviously pleased with himself. "As I said, we're going to have a little chat."

She turned her face away, as much to hide her tears

as to rebuke him. "I don't have anything to say to you."

"Fine. Then I'll do all the talking." He shifted to a more comfortable position. "I know you're upset about Skinner's article."

"Upset!" she cried. "I'm—"

He pressed a finger against her lips, silencing her. "Okay, maybe *upset* is too mild a word. You're mad. Furious. Outraged." He drew his finger away to catch a tear that had escaped and brought it to his tongue. The action made fresh tears surge to her eyes.

"And I don't blame you," he said softly, stroking her cheek. "Skinner was wrong to print what he did. Morally wrong, if not legally. But don't you see?" he said, his voice as well as his expression growing earnest. "Knuckling under to his pressure, and refusing to see me or talk to me, only gives him more power. He comes out the winner in this deal, not us. Ah, Suzy," he murmured, catching another tear that slipped from the corner of her eye. "I'd do anything to make this less painful. To spare you any embarrassment or humiliation. But I won't give you up. That's the one thing I can't do."

She gulped, trying to swallow back the emotion, the tears. "He'll win anyway. If I agree to see you, then he'll make the connection and he'll ruin you politically." Unable to hold back the tears any longer, she let them fall. "I don't want to cause you problems, Gil. I'd do anything to keep you from being hurt because of me."

He swept a hand across her cheek and leaned to

press his lips to hers. "Then stand beside me. We'll face them together and offer them the truth. If we rob them of the ammunition they might use against us by revealing it first, then we leave them powerless and with nothing left with which to hurt us." With a hand framed at her cheek, he slipped off her, then gathered her close to his side. "We can beat them at their own game, Suzy. Together we can beat them."

Suzy believed him. God help her, but she believed him and wanted to take that stand with him. But she couldn't. Not when this involved her mother, too. Not without first talking to her mother and preparing her for what might come.

"I need to talk to my mother first." She lifted her head to meet his gaze. "They'll drag her name into this along with ours. I won't do that to her. Not without discussing it with her first."

He drew her head back to his shoulder and pressed his lips against her hair. "Then talk to her. First thing in the morning. I'll go with you, if you want."

She closed her eyes and shook her head, already dreading the confrontation. "No. I need to do this alone."

Six

Suzy slept curled against Gil's side, not waking until he stirred just before dawn. Knowing that he had to leave before her neighbors started awakening, she rose with him, holding the front door open just wide enough for him to slip outside.

On the porch he turned back and touched a finger to his lips then to hers. The thoughtfulness in the gesture, the tenderness with which he then cupped his hand at her cheek and stroked a thumb beneath her eye, touched a place in her heart that had never been penetrated before.

"Call me," he whispered.

Then he was gone, leaping off her porch and jogging across the lawn to disappear into the darkness. She closed the door against the loss and turned her back to it, tears filling her eyes. She loved him, she realized, the pain like a fist twisting in her chest.

And, oh, God, how she hated to ask her mother to suffer the indignities that her loving him would surely demand.

Anxious to get the meeting with her mother behind her, she showered and dressed quickly, leaving her house just as her neighbors began to depart for work. Without any traffic to slow her, she made the trip to Elgin in less than twenty minutes. She parked her van in her mother's driveway and sank back in the seat, staring at the house they'd shared for thirteen years, before Suzy had left to strike out on her own.

Though early-morning sunlight washed over the small frame structure, staining the weathered wood a soft, warm gold, the house still managed to look shabby, abandoned, as lifeless as the woman who inhabited it.

As Suzy stared, her vision blurred by tears, she realized all that her mother had sacrificed when she'd divorced the reverend. Not only a husband and the love of her life, but a lifestyle that had provided her with a grand and elegantly decorated home in Dallas, designer clothes enough to fill a dozen closets and friends who dropped by at all hours of the day, competing for her attention.

And now she had this, Suzy reflected sadly. A rundown house in a rundown neighborhood. Clothes ordered from a discount catalogue, because she refused to go out shopping, fearing someone might recognize her if she dared. And no one to relieve the unrelenting passage of time, the loneliness that clung to the house like a shroud.

The reverend's infidelities and greed had stripped Sarah Swain of all she'd once held dear, including her emotional well-being.

And now Suzy was here to ask her to suffer it all again.

Suzy carefully timed telling her mother about Gil, knowing that anything unexpected or shocking might send her mother into an almost catatonic state. She greeted her mother in much the same way as she did at every visit. Pressing a kiss to her pale cheek with its paper-thin skin, asking about her health, her activities since their last visit. She waited until they were seated at the kitchen table, sharing a cup of tea before first broaching the subject of Gil.

"I've met someone, Mother."

"That's nice, dear."

Though her mother had responded, Suzy could tell by the way she continued to mindlessly move her spoon through her tea that she hadn't really heard what Suzy had said.

She laid her hand over her mother's, stopping her idle stirring. "Mother," she repeated, "I've met someone."

Sarah glanced up. "A man?"

Suzy nodded, her lips trembling in a smile. "Yes. A very nice man."

"You've never mentioned meeting anyone before. Is this serious?"

Suzy hesitated, unused to sharing her feelings, even with her own mother. "Yes. I think it is."

"Then you must bring him here. I'd like to meet the young man who's won my daughter's heart."

Tears filled Suzy's throat at the request, shamed by her earlier reluctance for Gil to meet her mother. She squeezed her mother's hand, saddened as always by the delicacy of the bone structure, the weakness in the fingers that had once held hers so tightly, so confidently, as together they'd skipped down the winding staircase in their home in Dallas. "I will, Mother. Soon. I promise."

They sat a moment in silence, Suzy watching her mother's face, while her mother stared at her tea, her mind already drifting to only God knew where.

"Mother?"

Sarah glanced up and blinked. "I'm sorry, dear. Were you saying something?"

"That I would bring the man I've met for a visit."

"Oh, yes. Do. I'll bake a cake."

Suzy wondered if tomorrow her mother would even remember that her daughter had been there for a visit, much less recall that she'd promised to bake a cake when Suzy returned with Gil. "Mother, there's something I need to ask you."

"All right, dear."

Suzy peered at her mother intently, as if in doing so she could will her mind to clear, to remain focused. "The man I've met is the governor of Texas."

Her mother stared at her a moment, then her jaw

slowly went slack. "The governor of Texas? Oh, my, Suzy, that's quite...impressive."

"Yes, it is," she said carefully. "But, Mother, you must understand that my seeing him will surely draw attention. Because of his position, people will want to know who I am. My background."

If possible her mother's face paled even more. "Oh, Suzy," she murmured, her voice quavering. "Must you tell them everything?"

Suzy tightened her grip on her mother's hand. "That's why I'm here. If left up to me, I'd tell them nothing. But there are those who won't accept me at face value. They'll dig into my past, and eventually they will find the connection. Right now, no one knows of my association with Gil. But for us to continue to see each other, I have to know that you're prepared for whatever might follow, because what affects me will affect you, as well."

Her mother stared at her, her face drawn, her lips trembling, looking years older and much more feeble than a woman of her age should. But when she spoke, it was with a clarity, a strength that Suzy hadn't witnessed in a long, long time.

"Do you love him?"

Tears filled Suzy's eyes. "Yes, I think I do."

"And does he love you?"

"I think so, though it's really too soon to say. We've known each other such a short time."

"Then we must do whatever is necessary for you to be with him." Smiling softly, she laid her hand over their joined hands and squeezed. "There is no greater gift we have to offer another than our love, and no greater responsibility than accepting love in return. Cherish it, honor it, but most importantly never dishonor the gift that is given to you. If you remember these things and practice them every day, happiness will be yours, no matter what trials may come your way.''

Suzy reached for the receiver, then jerked back her hand, frowning at the phone as she wiped her damp palm down her thigh. He'd said to call him, she told herself for the third time. But making the call meant stepping out of the safe world she'd created for herself and into his, exposing herself to those who surrounded him and to the press. It meant swimming with him in the fishbowl in which he lived.

She snatched up the phone. "So you'll grow fins," she muttered as she quickly punched in the number he'd left a zillion times on her answering machine. A female voice answered on the first ring.

"Governor Riley's office."

She gulped, her fingers growing slick on the receiver. "May...may I speak with Governor Riley, please."

"I'm sorry. The governor is in a meeting. Would you like to leave a message?"

Suzy hesitated a moment, wondering what type of message to leave and how much information she dared reveal. All systems are go? Mother gave us her blessings?

In the end, she simply blurted, "Tell him Suzy called," and hung up.

Clutching a hand at her knotted stomach, she turned from the phone, then spun back to stare at it in surprise when it rang. Cautiously she picked up the receiver. "Hello?"

"Hi."

She pressed a hand over her heart, sagging as the warmth in the familiar drawl spilled through her.

"Suzy? Are you there?"

She snapped to attention. "Yes. I'm here." Then she sagged again, laughing. "I was just surprised to hear your voice. I called less than a minute ago, and your secretary said you were in a meeting."

"That's the standard line she delivers. A way to screen my calls. Have you talked to your mother?"

She heard the anxiousness in his voice and smiled at it. Hugging the phone to her ear, she sank down on the sofa and stretched out, pillowing her head on a cushion. "Yes."

"And?"

She laughed, delighted by the impatience she heard in his reply. "We have her blessings." The sigh of relief that passed through the phone wires made her wish she were close enough to hug him. "So what do we do now?"

"Besides making wild passionate love?"

She laughed again. "Yes, besides that."

"We begin."

Begin? Shivers chased down her spine at all the simple word represented. A beginning with Gil. The possibility of a future together. "When can I see you?" she asked, suddenly anxious to see him, to touch him.

"What are you doing right now?"

Startled, she glanced around. "Nothing. Just lying on the sofa."

"Are you dressed?"

"Well, yes," she said, then frowned. "Why?"

"Get undressed. I'm on my way."

She sat up, scraping back her hair. "But, Gil—" There was a click, then a dial tone. Pulling the phone from her ear, she stared at it, then sank back against the cushions, the receiver hugged between her breasts. And laughed.

Suzy sat in the middle of her bed with the covers gathered to her waist, watching as Gil dressed. "A press conference?" she repeated, suddenly feeling nauseous. "Today?"

"Yep." He buckled his belt, then sank down on the edge of the bed and reached for his boots. "I figure the longer we wait to make some kind of announcement, the more time we're giving Skinner to dig the information out on his own." He tugged on one boot and glanced over his shoulder to wink at her. "But don't worry. You don't have to be there."

She slumped forward, dropping her forehead against her knees. "Thank God."

He laughed and reached to ruffle her hair. "Chicken."

She lifted her head. "Cluck. Cluck."

Chuckling, he pulled on his other boot, then stood, stomping his feet to shake his pants down over the heels. "Okay, Chicken Little, I'll call you and let you know what time I'll be on." He braced a hand on the mattress and leaned across it to kiss her. He drew back and pressed a fingertip against her lips, his smile growing tender. "It's going to be okay, Suzy. I promise you. Everything's going to be okay."

"Six o'clock news."

Suzy clutched the phone tighter to her ear. "Tonight?"

"Yeah, tonight. I've got to go and get ready. Wish me luck."

"You know I do. And, Gil," she added before he could hang up.

"Yes?"

She hesitated a moment, wanting desperately to tell him that she loved him. Instead she whispered, "Thank you," and replaced the receiver.

After hanging up, she looked at the clock, then around her kitchen, knowing that she'd go crazy if she had to stay in her house all afternoon, waiting for the press conference to air. On sudden inspiration she raced for the stairs and to her room, then out of her house, slinging a tote bag over her shoulder.

Two hours later she stepped back and critically eyed her work. "Well, what do you think?"

Her gaze on the hand mirror Suzy had given her, Celia stared at her reflection, "Is that really me?" was all she could manage.

Suzy laughed. "Well, of course it's you, silly. With a few enhancements, of course."

Celia touched a tentative hand to the shoulder-length wig Suzy had brought her, then ran a fingertip across her eyebrow, admiring the gold sparkles that glittered on the lid beneath it. She turned to look at Suzy, her smile radiant. "Wow. I look really cool."

Suzy rolled the cart out of the way and sat down on the edge of the bed. "Better than cool. You look positively outrageous."

"Think Gil will like my new look?"

Suzy wrinkled her nose and shook her head. "Probably not. He claims to like his women natural."

Celia glanced back at her reflection in the mirror, the excitement melting from her face. "Not when natural looks like a creature from a sci-fi movie."

Unable to bear the sadness in the girl's voice, Suzy scooted to sit beside her and slipped an arm around her shoulders. "There's nothing wrong with the way you look."

"Yeah," Celia replied miserably. "All the guys go for bald-headed girls."

"I don't know," Suzy replied. "A shaved head sure didn't hurt Demi Moore's looks *or* her popularity with the men."

Celia gave herself a closer inspection, then set aside the mirror and sank back against the pillow beside Suzy with a smile. "You're right. Bald *is* beautiful." She dug an elbow into Suzy's ribs. "Who knows? I might even make the cover of *Vogue*."

Laughing, Suzy hugged Celia to her side, then

glanced at the television where the news played on the screen, minus the accompanying sound. She quickly reached for the controls and turned up the volume. "It's time," she said, and reached for Celia's hand. "The news conference is about to start."

Celia squeezed her fingers around Suzy's, watching with her as Gil walked out the front door of the governor's mansion and crossed the porch, stopping before a podium lined with microphones.

"God, he's gorgeous," Suzy whispered. "And would you look at him? He's so calm!"

"Shh," Celia shushed. "I can't hear what he's saying."

Catching her lower lip between her teeth, Suzy forced herself to concentrate on Gil's voice and not on his face and her own stretched nerves.

"…elected by the people of this great state to fulfill the duties of governor. That is, and will continue to be, my focus until my term of office has ended.

"While campaigning for this position, I had the opportunity to meet many of you in person. Others I've spoken with on the phone or communicated with by letter. The man you met and conversed with, the man you elected as your governor, is just that. A man. A man with the same hopes and dreams shared by many of you. A man with the same rights guaranteed to each of you by the constitution of the United States. Among those is the right to life, liberty and the pursuit of happiness."

Firming his lips, he closed his hands around the sides of the podium. "Well, last week my rights were challenged. An article appeared in the newspaper, which I felt was inflammatory, unnecessary and certainly unkind to the parties involved." He lifted a hand as if to stave off an argument. "Now I know that our constitution also guarantees freedom of speech and press. But was that freedom written and fought for to hurt people? To allow one person to raise doubts about another person's character? To skew the facts for the sole purpose of entertainment?"

Shaking his head, he dropped his hands from the sides of the podium. "I don't think they were. I believe they were established to protect *all* people, not as a shield for a few to hide behind while they hurl accusations at the innocent. The constitution protects everyone. Elected officials, movie stars, singers, professional athletes. Everyone," he repeated, and brought his fist down on the podium for emphasis.

"I do not believe that these rights give public figures permission to behave improperly. But they do entitle them to a life separate from their chosen career. A normal life that allows them to make a few mistakes, to do things without having to worry about the rest of the world seeing it reported on television or reading about it in the newspaper the next day."

He paused, and a smile tugged at one corner of his mouth, as if he were amused by some private joke. When he spoke again, his voice was softer, a little sheepish. "I think most of you are aware that I'm single. And not for the reasons you might have heard or read," he added, arching a brow. "I'm single because I've never met a woman I'd consider spending the rest of my life with.'' He inhaled deeply, then shook his head as he released the breath. ''At least, I hadn't until recently.''

Suzy gasped, her fingers gripping Celia's.

''But I've met someone,'' he continued, unaware that Suzy's heart was threatening to pound right out of her chest. ''Someone whom I truly enjoy being with. Someone with whom I'd like to spend *more* time. She owns a local catering business here in Austin. Her name is Suzy Crane. Or at least that's the name she's gone by since she was about six. Prior to that time, her last name was Swain. Her father is the Reverend Bobby Swain.''

He paused again, as if to give the listeners a chance to absorb the importance of that name.

''For those of you who might not be familiar with Reverend Swain, he was a television evangelist who was involved in a scandal about twenty years ago that was widely reported by the media. Before it was over, the reverend's wife divorced him, changed her name and moved with their daughter to another town, in hopes of protecting her child from any more unsavory press. After a while the public forgot about the scandal...or they did until the reverend was indicted nine years later for misappropriating his ministry's funds. Then it started all over again. But the media wasn't satisfied with reporting the reverend's current misdeeds. No, they had to dig up the old scandal, as well. And although Suzy and her mother were no longer involved with the reverend, hadn't had any contact with him since the divorce, their names were dragged through the mud a second time, right along with the reverend's."

He gripped his hands on the podium and looked directly into the camera, and seemingly into the eyes and hearts of every viewer. "Now I ask you. Was that necessary? Was it even fair? Was it respecting those two ladies' right to life, liberty and the pursuit of happiness?" He lifted his hands from the podium and into the air. "Well, of course it wasn't. Simply by association, they were tried and convicted right along with him, their lives torn apart a second time. Wounds that had taken years to heal were ripped open and exposed for the world to gawk at and whisper about. Memories best forgotten were splashed across the front page of every newspaper in the country and headlined every television news program to haunt them again."

He firmed his lips. "I don't want that to happen a third time. I don't want to see Suzy's and her mother's names dragged through the dirt. But because of my position and my involvement with her, I'm afraid that's exactly what will happen. And that's why I'm here this evening, telling you all this, bearing my soul as well as Suzy's. I want you to hear it from me, from us, before you read about it in the newspaper or hear it on the news. Before the truth becomes so twisted you can't distinguish fact from speculation."

He began to slowly gather his notes. "From the cradle my parents taught me never to judge a person unless I'd first walked in their shoes. They taught me, too, that a person's appearance can be deceiving, that

I needed to look beyond the clothes they wore or the color of their skin and judge them by their actions, the size of their heart.''

He slipped his notes into his breast pocket, then braced his hands onto the lectern and looked directly into the camera again. ''And that's what I hope each of you will do. I hope you'll weigh carefully what you read or hear on television. Take the time to weigh the evidence and make decisions for yourself and not let others make them for you. And I hope, too, that from this point forward you'll demand honesty from the media, a return to integrity in reporting the news. Perhaps even compassion. There's a lot of good that goes on this world of ours, much of it unreported. Please don't allow anyone to force feed you only the bad. Demand the good and watch it grow.'' He stepped back from the podium and lifted a hand in farewell. ''Thank you for your time. Good night.''

The program cut to a commercial, but Suzy continued to stare at the screen, transfixed. ''Oh, my gosh,'' she murmured, drawing a hand to her heart. ''He was wonderful. Absolutely wonderful.'' She twisted her head around to look at Celia. ''Didn't you think he was great?''

The makeup Suzy had applied to Celia's face was running in rivulets down the young girl's cheeks. ''The best. Oh, Suzy,'' she said, and flung her arms around Suzy's neck. ''You're so lucky to have a man like Gil to love you.''

Suzy wrapped her arms around Celia and turned her gaze to the screen where the news program had resumed, blinking back tears. ''Yeah, I know.''

Seven

After she returned home from the hospital, Suzy's phone rang off the wall. It seemed everyone she knew—and some she didn't—had seen Gil's press conference and called to offer their support and congratulations. Between calls, she managed to place one to her mother

"Mother? It's Suzy. Did you watch the press conference?"

"Yes, dear. David and I watched it together."

"David?" Suzy repeated, tensing. "David who?"

"Well, I don't recall his last name. Just a minute and I'll ask."

"Mother, wait!" Suzy cried, wondering if her mother was hallucinating or if she did in fact have a total stranger in her house. But it was too late. She could already hear her mother calling to someone in the other room.

"Langerhan," her mother replied, returning to the phone. "David Langerhan. It was so nice of Gil to send him over to watch the program with me."

"Gil sent him?" Suzy repeated, her concerns in no way appeased.

"Yes. He was afraid that after the news conference aired the press might attempt to contact me, so he sent one of his men over. It really wasn't necessary," her mother added, lowering her voice, "though I have enjoyed his company."

Suzy couldn't decide whether she should jump into her van and race to her mother's house or call the police. Trying to think rationally, she asked, "Could I speak with David, please?"

"Certainly, dear." She heard her mother cover the mouthpiece with her hand, then her muffled voice as she called the mysterious David to the phone.

There was a rustle of movement as the phone changed hands, then a male voice. "Hi, Suzy."

She all but wilted onto the sofa. "Dave," she said in relief, recognizing the voice of Gil's bodyguard. "I'm sorry. I didn't realize it was you with Mother. When she said she'd watched the press conference with David, I thought—" She laughed weakly. "Never mind what I thought. Is Mother all right?"

"Best I can tell. No one has called or come by, which is a good sign, I'd think."

"Yes. That is a good sign. How long do you plan to stay?"

"As long as she wants me. Those were Gil's instructions."

"If you need to leave, I can come and stay with her."

"No need. I've got things covered here. In fact, I really need to go. It's my turn at Scrabble."

Suzy's eyebrows shot up. "You're playing Scrabble with my mother?"

"Yeah," he replied, and sighed heavily. "And she's beating my socks off. Is there such a word as mbira?"

Suzy laughed. "I haven't the faintest idea. Why don't you challenge her and see for yourself?"

"Already missed two turns doing that. Listen, I gotta go. The longer I take for my turn, the more time I'm giving her to come up with another word to stump me."

"Go on and play then," she said, laughing. "Tell mother I'll talk to her later."

As she replaced the phone, there was a knock at her door. Praying it wasn't the press, she tiptoed to the door and peered through the peephole. Seeing Gil on her front porch, she threw the door wide. She was in his arms before he had time to brace himself.

Knocked off balance, he staggered back a step, wrapping his arms around her to steady them both. "Hey. What's this all about?"

With her arms linked behind his neck, she smiled at him. "You are undoubtedly the sweetest, most thoughtful man I've ever known."

Chuckling, he lifted her higher on his chest and

walked them both inside the house, kicking the door closed behind them. "And how did you come to that conclusion?"

"I just talked to Mother. And Dave," she added. "I was so wrapped up in myself, I didn't even think about her watching the program alone. But you did," she said and drew his face down to hers. "And that was so, so sweet," she whispered against his lips.

Moaning, he tightened his arms around her and backed toward the sofa. When his legs bumped the cushions, he dropped down and shifted her across his lap. He slowly withdrew his mouth from hers and wound a stray lock of hair behind her ear. "I have a confession," he admitted reluctantly. "It wasn't my idea."

Puzzled, Suzy sat back. "Whose was it?"

"Dave's. He asked me if your mother lived alone, and when I told him she did, he offered to drive over and sit with her."

"Well then, Dave's sweet. But so are you," she insisted. and hugged him. "I can't remember ever hearing a more moving speech. You were wonderful. Celia thought so, too."

Bracing his hands at her waist, he pushed back to look at her. "Celia? You were at the hospital?"

Embarrassed by her cowardice to watch the program alone, she wrinkled her nose. "Yeah. I knew I'd go stir-crazy if I stayed here all afternoon, so I went to visit Celia and watch the press conference with her."

"How was she?"

She lifted a shoulder and fussed with the knot of his tie, avoiding his gaze. "About the same, I guess. We played beauty shop. I loaned her one of my wigs and did her makeup for her."

"The red one you wore to the dedication?"

"No. Blond. Her coloring is all wrong for a red-head."

Gil bumped his nose against hers. "And you think I'm sweet? You're the sweet one."

Suzy melted against his chest. "Want to fight about it?"

"No way."

A buzzing sound had them drawing apart again. Suzy frowned as Gil slipped a hand into his jacket. He withdrew his cell phone with an apologetic smile. "Sorry. I had it set to vibrate, instead of ring." He pressed a button and lifted the phone to his ear. "Gil."

He listened a moment, his gaze on Suzy. "I would've called first, but there just wasn't time." He waited, then said patiently, "Yes, Mom, I know it must have come as a surprise to you. But it couldn't be helped." A smile spread across his face. "I'm with her now." Another pause, then, "Sure. We can be there in an hour." Pulling the phone from his ear, he disconnected the call.

Suzy eased back on his lap. "We can be where?"

"At my parents'. They want to meet you."

She leaped to her feet. "Your parents!" she cried. "But I can't meet them now."

Gil stood. "Why not?"

"Because it's late and it would take me hours to get ready, that's why."

"You're fine just as you are."

"But look at me!" she cried, holding out her arms so that he could get a good look at the faded jeans and baggy denim shirt she'd worn to the hospital. "I can't meet your parents dressed like this!"

Chuckling, he slipped his arms around her waist and drew her to him. "My parents will like you no matter what you're wearing."

And he'd been right. His parents had seemed to like her. And Suzy had liked them. They were both as down-to-earth and unassuming as their son. Within minutes of her and Gil's arrival, his parents had put her at ease, their friendliness and warmth quickly dispelling all her uncertainties about meeting them.

"I just hope this meeting goes as well," she murmured to her reflection the following morning, as she checked her appearance one last time in her compact mirror. She plucked at the collar of her oversize cream silk blouse, then smoothed a hand down the side of the black leather skirt she'd selected to wear to the brunch, praying that the outfit was suitable. Though she'd spent more than half her life trying to dress like anyone other than a preacher's kid, today she'd have given almost anything to have something more sedate to wear.

With a resigned sigh she replaced her compact and opened the door.

The woman behind the desk glanced up, then rose,

smiling as she extended a hand in greeting. "You must be Suzy. I'm Mary, Gil's secretary. It's so nice to finally meet you. I've heard so much about you."

Suzy shook her hand. "Thank you…I think."

Mary laughed easily. "It was all nice, I assure you."

Suzy blew a breath up at her bangs. "Whew. That's a relief."

"Gil has some gentlemen in his office. Can I get you a cup of coffee or a soft drink while you wait?"

"Coffee, if you don't mind," Suzy replied, hoping the caffeine would steady her nerves.

Mary hurried for the door. "I'll be just a minute. Make yourself at home," she said, gesturing toward a grouping of chairs.

Too nervous to sit, Suzy prowled the office, stopping before a coffee table to flip through the magazines scattered across its top.

"Dang it," she muttered as some slipped to the floor. She stooped to pick up the periodicals, started to replace them, but froze when her gaze fell on the headline of the newspaper the dropped magazines had exposed: The Governor's Favorite Dish. The words swirled before her eyes, while her stomach churned sickly as she stared at the accompanying photo someone had secretly snapped of her and Gil standing beside her van the night they'd first met.

The sound of voices carried from Gil's office, and she quickly dropped the magazines over the newsprint, covering the hideous headline. Sure that the men with him were there to discuss the newspaper's most recent attack on Gil, she glanced toward the door, straining to hear as it opened.

"I'm warning you, Gil," she overheard a man say, his voice raised in anger. "You're making a big mistake. Whether or not what the press is saying about this woman is true doesn't matter. She'll poison your career. Mark my word. You'll lose every bit of support you've managed to get, because of her."

The blood draining from her face, Suzy took a step back, sickened even more by what she'd overheard.

"Now wait just a damn minute, Henry," she heard Gil say.

The door slammed shut, obviously closed by Gil to block the man's departure, and Suzy couldn't hear any more of the conversation. But she didn't need to hear any more. She whirled for the door to the hallway, desperate to escape before she was seen.

Just as she reached for the knob, the door opened and Mary breezed in, bobbling the cup of steaming coffee when she bumped into Suzy.

"Oh, my goodness," she said in dismay, and darted around Suzy to set the cup on the desk. She snatched a tissue from a container and dabbed at the hot coffee that had splashed onto her sleeve. "I didn't spill any on you, did I?" she asked, glancing Suzy's way in concern.

Suzy shook her head. "No. No, you didn't."

Mary tilted her head, her brows drawing together. "Are you all right? You look so pale."

"Actually," Suzy said, pressing a trembling hand to her forehead. "I do feel rather ill. Would you mind telling Gil that I had to leave? And tell him...tell him that I'm sorry.''

Suzy lay on her bed with a washcloth pressed to her forehead and the drapes drawn to block out the sunlight. She welcomed the dark. Needed it to hide in.

Feeling the tears coming again, she rolled to her side and dragged the washcloth down to cover her mouth, trying to force back the regret. She'd known this would happen. She'd tried to warn Gil that he would be hurt if he insisted upon continuing their relationship.

The telephone rang, but she ignored it, just as she had each time it had rung since she'd returned home from the governor's mansion more than two hours before.

Clutching the cloth to her mouth, she let the tears fall, knowing that she couldn't see or talk to him again. For his own good, she'd end this once and for all.

With meetings scheduled back-to-back all day, Gil could do nothing but dial Suzy's number in between sessions and listen to it ring. He considered sending Mary over to check on her, but decided against it, fearing her presence would make Suzy feel uncomfortable, since she didn't know his secretary. He racked his brain, trying to think of a friend Suzy had mentioned whom he might call, and suddenly remembered her visiting with Erik Thompson's wife at the dedication.

Flipping open his Rolodex, he looked up Erik's number and punched it in. He breathed a sigh of relief when Penny answered after the first ring.

"Hi, Penny. Gil Riley. Listen, I need a favor. Suzy was here earlier, but had to leave unexpectedly because she became ill."

"Oh, dear," Penny said in concern. "What's wrong with her?"

Gil dragged a hand over his already-mussed hair. "I don't know. I've called several times to check on her but only get her answering machine. I'd drive over, but I'm stuck in meetings all day."

"I'll go," Penny offered. "Do you want me to call you and let you know how she's doing?"

Relieved, Gil sank back in his chair. "Would you? I'd sure appreciate it."

"Suzy?"

At the sound of Penny's voice, Suzy groaned and dragged the pillow over her head.

"Suzy! Are you up here?"

Regretting having given Penny a key to her house, Suzy shoved the pillow away, knowing her friend wouldn't leave until she responded. "I'm in my bedroom!" she shouted.

Penny appeared in the doorway. "Are you sick?" she asked hesitantly.

Suzy pulled the pillow across her stomach and hugged it to her. "Yeah. Sorta."

"Gosh. It's dark in here. Mind if I turn on the light?"

Suzy pushed out a hand. "No. Please don't. My head is killing me."

Penny eased closer to the bed. "Can I get you anything?"

"No. I'll be fine."

Pursing her lips at Suzy's stubbornness, Penny headed for the bathroom. "I bet an aspirin would make you feel better."

"Really, Penny. I don't need—" Suzy dropped her head to the mattress in frustration as Penny disappeared beyond the bathroom door.

"Gil called," Penny said from the other room. "He's worried about you."

Suzy set her jaw, determined not to cry. "There's nothing to worry about. I told you, I'm fine."

"Good heavens, Suzy," Penny fussed. "You've got enough toothpaste in here to keep a small town supplied for a year."

"Quit digging through my drawers," Suzy grumped irritably.

"I'm not digging. I'm looking for the aspirin."

"It's in the medicine cabinet on the wall. Right next to my birth control pills." Muttering under her breath, Suzy punched a pillow up beneath her head and settled back to wait, resigned to being coddled.

"Suzy?"

"What?"

"Have you quit taking your birth control pills?"

Suzy pushed up, bracing herself on her hands as

Penny returned from the bathroom. "Of course not. Why?"

Penny reached to switch on the lamp, murmured "sorry" when Suzy threw up a hand to cover her eyes, then sat down on the side of the bed and held open the container. "We've always been on the same cycle, but your dispenser still has pills in it, and I finished mine almost a week ago."

Her blood chilling, Suzy snatched the container from Penny's hand to examine it herself. "Are you sure?"

"I'm positive. I'm very careful about taking my pills. Erik and I want to wait at least another year before we start our family."

Suzy rubbed her temple, trying to remember. "I know I took one this morning. And yesterday, too." She dropped her hand, remembering. "But I didn't take any when I was at the ranch with Gil," she said, lifting her head to look at Penny, her face pale. "I didn't have them with me."

"You only missed taking two?"

Suzy glanced down at the dispenser realizing she should have started her period by now. "No. Three. I didn't take one the following Monday, either."

"Why not?"

Suzy curled her fingers around the container. "Because I forgot," she snapped. "Okay?"

Penny dropped her gaze, and Suzy immediately regretted the sharp words. She tossed the container aside and caught her friend's hand. "I'm sorry, Pen.

I didn't mean to take it out on you. It's just been a really rotten day."

Penny smiled in understanding and squeezed her hand. "Probably made worse because you don't feel well."

It was Suzy's turn to drop her gaze. "I'm not really sick," she mumbled. "I just used that as an excuse to leave the mansion."

Penny's jaw sagged. "You mean you lied to Gil?"

Suzy nodded slowly.

Penny snatched her hand from hers. "You ought to be ashamed of yourself," she scolded. "He's been worried sick about you."

Suzy firmed her lips, knowing she'd done the right thing. "It couldn't be helped."

"Well, of course it could," Penny argued. "You could have just told him the truth if you didn't want to attend the brunch with him."

Suzy shook her head, the tears starting all over again. "No, I couldn't. Not without telling him what I overheard."

Penny leaned closer. "What did you overhear?"

Suzy caught up the edge of the sheet and dabbed at her eyes. "When I got there, there were some men in Gil's office, and I heard one of them shouting. He said that I was poison. That if Gil continued to see me, Gil would lose all his support for the legislation he wants to see passed."

"That's simply not true!" Penny argued. "There's no way you could harm Gil's effectiveness. Not after that press conference he held last night."

"But I already have! Didn't you see the headline in this morning's paper?"

"Well, no. I didn't have time to read the paper."

"'The Governor's Favorite Dish,'" Suzy quoted bitterly. "Big, bold type right on the front page. And the people I was to have brunch with are his *supporters,* his friends, the people who are supposed to be on his side. If even one of them questions Gil's effectiveness because of me, then I've done exactly what that man accused me of doing. I've poisoned his career." Dragging a hand across her wet cheek, she shook her head. "I've got to end this before any real harm is done."

"Oh, Suzy," Penny murmured worriedly. "Talk to Gil first. Tell him what you overheard. There's always the chance that you misinterpreted what the man said, or perhaps even what he was talking about."

"No," Suzy said, shaking her head. "I didn't misinterpret anything. I heard every word clear as a bell."

"Talk to him anyway," Penny urged. "Give him a choice in the decision. After all, you aren't in this alone."

Suzy dropped her gaze to the dispenser of birth control pills again and her stomach took another nauseating turn. "Penny, do you think it's possible to get pregnant if you forget to take a couple of pills?"

Penny's forehead creased in concern. "I don't know. Maybe."

Drawing in a long breath, Suzy slowly forced it out, then glanced up at Penny. "Would you mind going to the drugstore for me and buying one of those home pregnancy kits?''

Though Suzy loved Penny dearly, she sent her friend home after Penny had returned with the pregnancy test. What she had to do was private. Personal. The results a secret that must be guarded more closely than any of the others Suzy had kept through the years. And though Suzy trusted Penny implicitly, she didn't want to burden her friend with yet another secret of hers to protect.

Thus, Suzy was alone when she learned the results of the test. Sitting on the closed toilet seat, she stared at the colored strip through a blur of tears.

I can't be, she told herself, gulping. After missing only a few days' medication? Surely a few measly pills couldn't affect the drug's ability to prevent a pregnancy?

But the evidence was there before her eyes. Whether the fault was placed on three missed pills or Suzy was simply a statistic, one of the minuscule percentage of women who became pregnant while taking birth control pills, the fact was she was going to have a baby.

And Governor Gil Riley was going to be a father.

Groaning, she dropped her forehead to the arm she'd braced along the edge of the sink. And she'd worried that the scandal surrounding her father would ruin Gil's career. Ha! That was nothing compared to the battering Gil's good name would take when news hit the streets that the governor had fathered a baby out of wedlock.

Slowly she raised her head. But they can't find out, she told herself. If anyone learned of this, Gil would be ruined!

She gripped her hands on the edge of the sink and pulled herself shakily to her feet. But no one knows, she reminded herself. No one but me. Lifting her head, she stared at her reflection in the mirror. And no one will ever know, she promised herself.

Penny's phone call, telling Gil that Suzy was fine, that she'd just suffered a small bout with an upset stomach, did little to reassure Gil. Especially when Suzy continued to allow her machine to pick up his phone calls. Frustrated and more than a little worried, he drove to her house once he'd completed his duties later that evening.

When he didn't get an answer to his knock at her front door, he headed around to the back and was surprised to see that her van was missing from the driveway. With his hand lifted to knock on the kitchen door, he heard someone call his name. Turning, he frowned, seeing no one.

"Governor? Is that you?"

He squinted his eyes against the darkness to peer at the dark ivy-draped fence that separated Suzy's drive from the house next door, where he was sure the voice had come. "Yes. Who's there?"

"It's me, Mrs. Woodley, Suzy's neighbor."

Shaking his head at the woman's nosiness, Gil

hopped down from the porch and crossed the drive. "Hello, Mrs. Woodley."

"I saw your press conference on television last night and I was so surprised to discover that you're dating my Suzy. We're very close," she added. "Why, she's just like a daughter to me."

Biting back a smile, Gil nodded, sure that Suzy would deny that relationship. "I'm sure that you are."

"Are you here to see her?" she asked.

"Yes, ma'am. But it doesn't appear that she's home."

"Oh, she isn't," the ever watchful Mrs. Woodley informed him. "She left over an hour ago. Watched her load her van from my bedroom window."

Gil frowned. "Load her van? I wasn't aware that she had an event to cater tonight."

"I don't believe she did. At least, I didn't see her load any trays of food or dishware into her van. Just suitcases."

Gil's frown deepened. "Suitcases?"

"Yes. Several. Must be going on a trip, because she even put the garbage out before she left, and pickup isn't for another two days." There was a short pause, then the woman added, sounding offended, "She usually lets me know when she's going to be away. Always asks me to keep an eye on her place for her. That's what neighbors are for, you know. We look out for each other."

"Yes, I'm sure you do," Gil replied vaguely, then asked, "Mrs. Woodley, could I ask a favor of you?"

"Why, yes, Governor," she replied, perking up. "I'd be honored."

"When Suzy returns, would you call me?" He slipped a card in the slit between two pickets. "The number to my cell phone is on this card."

Suzy sat at her mother's kitchen table, clasping her mother's hand in hers. "I know, Mother," she said. "I'll miss you, too, but it won't be for long. As soon as I get settled, you can come for a visit."

"Oh, I don't know, dear," her mother said uneasily. "I really don't like to travel, you know."

"But Dallas isn't that far. And if you don't want to drive, you could always take the bus."

"We'll see," her mother said vaguely, then tilted her head, tears welling up in her eyes as she looked at Suzy. "Are you sure you're doing the right thing? Shouldn't you talk to Gil about this first?"

Suzy dropped her mother's hand and rose to pace away. "I can't tell him about this, Mother. He would want to get married, and I won't let him ruin his life that way."

"Ruin?" her mother queried. "Marriage is meant to enhance lives, not ruin them."

Suzy whirled, her eyes blazing. "The way your life was enhanced by your marriage to the reverend?" Seeing her mother's stricken face, Suzy immediately regretted the unkind words. She went to her and dropped down on a knee, gathering her mother's hand in hers. "I'm sorry. That was mean and uncalled for."

"No," her mother said quietly. "You spoke the

truth. What was in your heart." She clasped Suzy's hand between hers. "But don't make the mistake of judging all marriages by your father's and mine. Give Gil a chance, Suzy. And give yourself a chance at happiness."

Eight

Gil didn't bother to call first before heading to Elgin and Suzy's mother's house. He figured if Suzy discovered he was on his way, she would just run again. He knew the trip might well be a waste of his time, but it was the only place left he knew to look for her.

Due to the lateness of the hour, traffic on the highway was light. With each set of headlights that appeared in the opposite lane, he watched the passing vehicle to make sure it wasn't Suzy on her way back to Austin.

As he drove, the same question played over and over through his mind. *Why?* What had happened to make her run this time? Though he racked his brain for an explanation for her sudden disappearance, the only answer he could come up with was that the head-line in the morning paper had upset her.

But surely Suzy hadn't expected the media's ha-rassment to end with the press conference? He'd known that some type of retaliation would follow his public address and thought she would, too.

A set of headlights appeared in the opposing lane and Gil narrowed his eyes, watching its fast approach. As the vehicle whisked past, Gil recognized the van as Suzy's. He stomped on the brakes and whipped the steering wheel to the left, spinning his truck around in the opposite direction. He pressed the accelerator to the floorboard and shot his truck across the grass median and onto the highway in pursuit.

Gaining on her, he flashed his headlights, signaling for her to stop. "Come on, Suzy," he muttered under his breath. "Pull over."

A set of headlights appeared behind Gil, seeming to come out of nowhere. He glanced at his rearview mirror and swore when he saw that it was a patrol car behind him. The deck of red lights on the car's roof flashed and a siren bleeped, signaling him to pull over. But Gil wasn't about to give up the chase and take a chance on losing Suzy again. Instead, he sped up and swerved into the fast lane. He pulled up along-side the van and glanced over. Their eyes met for only a brief second, but long enough for Gil to see the desperation, the fear, before she looked away and sped up.

Swearing under his breath, he took another glimpse in the rearview mirror and saw that the patrol car had followed him into the fast lane. In hopes of using the patrol car to block Suzy in, he pressed his foot down on the accelerator and shot past the van, swerving over into the lane in front of it. Slowly he eased on the brakes. With the patrol car on her left and the bar ditch on her right, she had no choice but to match her speed to his. He came to a complete stop, quickly jumped out and ran back to the van, which had stopped directly behind him. He yanked open the door.

"What the hell is wrong with you?" he shouted furiously. "Why didn't you stop when you saw me?"

Her face red with fury, Suzy reached for the door. "Because I don't want to see you. That's why."

Gil slammed a hand against the door, keeping her from shutting it, then moved into the space and grabbed her arm. "What's going on, Suzy? What's wrong?"

"Hold it right there, mister!"

Having forgotten about the highway patrolman, Gil groaned in frustration. "It's all right, officer. I was just trying to stop this lady."

"Please help me, officer," Suzy begged. "This man tried to run me off the road."

Gil slapped a hand against the side of the van in anger. "Damn it, Suzy! What are you trying to do? Get me arrested?"

He heard a pistol cock behind him.

"Put your hands on the side of the van and spread 'em."

"If you'll give me a minute," Gil said in frustration, "I can explain everything." Turning, he reached for his wallet in his hip pocket, intending to offer the patrolman his driver's license. But before he touched a finger to his wallet, a hand clamped down on his shoulder, and he was shoved roughly face-first against the side of the van.

"Now spread 'em," the patrolman ordered. "Are you all right, miss?" he asked Suzy as he jerked one of Gil's hands down and held it behind his back to slap a handcuff around his wrist.

"Yes. I'm fine," she replied, her voice quavering. "But I'd like to go, if that's all right."

"You don't want to press charges?'

"No. I just want to leave."

"Then go on. I'll see that he doesn't cause you any more trouble."

"Suzy!" Gil shouted as the officer clipped the second cuff into place, the sound echoing the van door slamming. The officer pulled him clear of the van and Suzy reversed quickly, then drove away, swinging over onto the shoulder to avoid hitting Gil's truck.

Furious with both Suzy and the patrolman, Gil tried to jerk free from the officer's grip. "The handcuffs aren't necessary," he growled. "I'm Governor Gil Riley."

"Yeah," the officer jeered as he shoved Gil toward the patrol car. "And I'm Bill Clinton. Get in," he ordered as he opened the rear door. "You and me are going for a little ride."

By the time Gil finished explaining that he wasn't trying to run Suzy off the road, but was only trying to stop her, and had provided those at the station with enough identification to prove that he really *was* the governor of Texas, as he'd claimed, Suzy was long gone.

But by that time Gil really didn't much want to see her, anyway. He was afraid if he did get within arm's reach of her, he might be tempted to wring her pretty neck. So instead of resuming his search, he drove back to Austin and to the governor's mansion and crawled wearily into bed.

Six hours later he was sitting at his breakfast table opposite his bodyguard and blowing on his coffee, while scanning the front page of the newspaper.

There were at least three different sidebars directing readers to stories in other sections, where details of the late-night car chase and his subsequent arrest were recorded. But not one of the articles mentioned a word about the charges against Gil being dropped or the patrolman's apology to Gil for the rough treatment he'd received and for not recognizing him right off.

No, instead the reporters had focused on the negative and the sensational, going into lengthy detail about how the governor was caught speeding in the middle of the night while trying to run his girlfriend off the road, following what appeared to be a domestic dispute between the two. They included reports of the highspeed police chase that ensued and painted a dramatic word picture of the patrolman overpowering Gil in order to handcuff him.

After reading all the articles, Gil tossed the paper aside in disgust. "If you take out all the speculation and hearsay," he told Dave angrily, "there wouldn't be enough copy left to fill three lines of print."

"Seldom is," Dave murmured, continuing to frown over the crossword puzzle he was working on.

Gil rose to refill his cup with coffee. "Making me out to be some kind of outlaw," he grumbled irritably. "You'd think they'd have better things to write about than what's going on in my personal life."

"I don't know, Governor. Lately your personal life's gotten pretty interesting."

Gil whipped his head around to light into Dave, but saw his bodyguard's crooked smile and snorted a laugh, his anger dissipating. "Yeah. I guess it has at that."

Dave set aside his puzzle. "A call came in earlier this morning from some lady." He pulled a slip of paper from his shirt pocket. "Gladys Woodley," he verified, then slipped the note back into his pocket. "Said she was Suzy's neighbor and you'd given her this number to call."

"I told her to call my *cell* phone," Gil said in frustration. "Not the mansion line. Did she say that she'd seen Suzy?"

"No. If she had, I would've roused you. But she did mention seeing someone snooping around Suzy's house this morning just before daylight."

Gil frowned as he sat back down at the table opposite Dave. "Did you check it out?"

"Yeah. But whoever was there was gone by the

time we arrived. There wasn't a sign of an attempted break-in. All they took was her garbage.''

"Her garbage?"

''Yeah. It's an old trick, used mostly by stalkers and burglars to gain information about the inhabitants of a residence. You'd be surprised what kind of information is revealed in the stuff a person throws out.''

Gil frowned in puzzlement. "Suzy never mentioned anything about anyone stalking her."

"If anyone was, she probably was never aware." Dave took a sip of his coffee. "Are you going to try to find her?"

Gil sank back in his chair, scowling. "I wouldn't know where to begin to look. I've already spoken with her mother. If she knows anything, she isn't talking. Same with her friend Penny."

Dave lifted a brow. "You do realize that you have other methods available to you?"

Gil shook his head. "I won't use the power of my office to track her down." His scowl deepened. "Besides, I'd be a fool to try to find her when she's made it more than clear that she doesn't want to see me again. As far as I'm concerned, it's over."

"How long do you plan to stay?"

Suzy lifted a shoulder at her friend Jon's question as she chopped vegetables alongside him in the kitchen of his Dallas-based restaurant. "A couple of months, maybe. I don't know. I just need a place to lay low for a while."

He angled his head to peer at her suspiciously. "Are you sure you aren't wanted by the law?"

A wan smile curved her lips. "No. It's nothing like that."

Shaking his head, Jon resumed his cutting. "The governor," he said, then snorted a laugh. "Imagine you hooked up with the governor of Texas."

"I'm not hooked up with him," Suzy replied irritably, then added in a low voice, "at least, I'm not any longer."

Jon gathered up the lettuce he'd shredded and dumped it into a large bowl. "Well, whatever the reason for your sudden appearance on my doorstep, I'm glad for the extra help. Good cooks are hard to come by these days." He poked an elbow at her ribs. "Besides, being your employer means I get to boss you around."

She waved her knife beneath his nose. "Just try it, big guy," she warned, "and you might find yourself boiling in the pot right along with these carrots."

He stumbled back a step, pretending fright. "You wouldn't dare."

"Try me."

Laughing, he held up his hands. "No way. I've seen how you can handle a knife. When we were taking those cooking classes together, everybody called you slasher. Remember?"

Relieved that she could still smile, in spite of the emotional turmoil her life was currently undergoing, Suzy scraped the cuttings into the disposal, then flipped the switch. "Yeah, I remember." As she watched the cuttings slide down the drain, her smile slowly faded. "Jon?"

"Yeah?"

"I don't want anyone to know I'm here. Okay?"

He moved to stand beside her and slipped an arm around her shoulders. "Whatever you say, Suzy."

"Several radio stations have run unofficial polls, and the results show that the majority of the people still support Gil."

"That's the public," the lieutenant governor reminded the men gathered around the conference table. "He's still taking a beating by the press."

"But it's the public's opinion that counts," another argued.

"Their voices are the ones the congressmen are going to listen to."

"*If* they bother to share their opinions with their congressmen," the lieutenant governor interjected. "But if they keep their opinions to themselves, it's the media who will influence the voting on current legislation."

Gil, who had remained silent throughout the discussion, rose. "Then we need to encourage our fellow Texans to call or write their congressmen. And not with their opinions about me," he added, meeting the gaze of each person in turn. "They need to let their opinions on the issues be known." He turned away from the table, dragging a hand over his hair. "That's what's important here. The issues. Not me or what's going on in my personal life. The focus should be on the laws being written and voted on, not on gossip.''

"Laws don't sell papers. Gossip does.''

At the muttered statement Gil stopped with his back to the group. He drew in a deep breath, trying to rein in the fury, then turned. "Then we shouldn't have a problem because there isn't anything more to gossip about. Not about me, anyway.''

"The word on the street is that the newspaper is going to break some big story about you in tomorrow's paper.''

"What story?'' Gil demanded angrily. "I haven't seen or talked to Suzy in over a week. Hell!'' he said, tossing up his hands. "I don't even know where she is!''

The person who had mentioned the story lifted a shoulder. "I don't know what it's supposed to be about. I'm just telling you what I heard.''

Gil glanced at his press agent. "Is there any way we can find out what they're planning to print?''

The man shook his head doubtfully. "I don't know. I can try.''

Gil set his jaw. "Then do it. And if it's a lie, by God this time I'm going to drag them through the courts.''

"On what basis?''

"Defamation of character.''

Jon entered the kitchen and crossed directly to Suzy. He tossed a newspaper on the countertop in front of her. "Have you seen this?''

Frowning, Suzy wiped her hands on her apron, then picked up the paper. In bold print across the top of the page was the headline: GOVERNOR DADDY?

She dropped the paper and turned to Jon, her face drained of color. "How could they know?" she whispered, then said more fiercely, "How could they possibly *know?* I didn't tell anyone, except my mother and she'd never talk to the press."

"Then it's true? You're really pregnant?"

Suzy whirled away, clamping a hand over her mouth as tears rose to choke her, imagining the shock Gil must have experienced when he saw the headline, the hurt and anger that would surely have followed when he realized that she'd kept her pregnancy a secret from him.

Jon touched her elbow. "Suzy? Is it true?"

She dropped her chin to her chest. "Yes," she said miserably.

"Does he know?"

Unable to speak, she shook her head.

"Damn," he swore.

She turned, her eyes flooded with tears. "I couldn't tell him. He would have insisted on getting married, then everyone would know he'd fathered a child out of wedlock and his career would've been ruined."

"Are you sure about that?"

"Well, of course I'm sure!" she cried. "The press had a field day, trying to destroy his image, when they discovered we were just dating." She gestured angrily at the paper. "And look what they've done to him now that it's rumored that I'm pregnant."

"But what they've printed is simply speculation," Jon reminded her, in an obvious attempt to calm her. "They never came right out and said the baby was his. They merely posed a question, suggesting that it is."

Suzy stared, her eyes widening, her mind whirling, an idea taking shape. "That's it," she whispered. "I can say the baby belongs to someone else, that I was already pregnant when I met Gil."

"They're not going to let you off that easy," Jon warned. "They're going to demand the name of the baby's father."

When Suzy remained silent, her gaze on Jon, he backed up a step and held up a hand. "Uh-uh. No way. You're not sticking me with this. Friendship only goes so far."

"Jon, please," she begged. "We don't have to get married or anything, and you don't have to truly be responsible for the baby. You just have to say that it's yours."

"But it's not!"

"I know it's not. And I wouldn't ask you if there was any other way out of this mess."

"There is another way," he reminded her firmly. "You can tell Gil about the baby. He's the one who got you into this mess. Not me."

Gil stared at the headline, after two hours still unable to believe what he was seeing. Suzy was pregnant? And with his child? He shook his head and dropped the paper to the breakfast table. "She can't be," he said to Dave. "She's on the pill. She told me so herself. This is nothing but a smear campaign, based on nothing but a pack of lies."

"Maybe. Maybe not."

"Well, of course it's lies," Gil shouted angrily. "She'd have told me if she were pregnant."

When Dave lifted a brow, Gil slumped back in his chair. "Okay," he said in defeat. "So maybe she wouldn't have told me. But I still don't believe she's pregnant. I specifically asked her if I needed to use protection, and she told me, no, she was on the pill."

A knock sounded at the back door, and Gil yelled impatiently, "The door's open."

His press agent entered. "Morning, Gil. Dave," he said, with a nod to both. He poured himself a cup of coffee and joined them at the table.

"What did you find out?" Gil asked.

"Not much," his press agent admitted regretfully. "No one is willing to reveal their source. But from what information I was able to gather, it seems the story was based on a home pregnancy kit found in Suzy's garbage."

Gil glanced at Dave, anger burning through him as he remembered the morning Mrs. Woodley had called to report someone snooping around Suzy's house. He looked back to his press agent. "Is that legal? Can anyone who wants to dig through your garbage and print a story on what they found there?"

His press agent slid an uneasy glance at Dave, then

looked down at his coffee. "There isn't a law against it that I know of. Once garbage is placed on the street, it's fair game for anyone who wants to rummage through it."

"That's ridiculous!"

"Ridiculous or not," Dave interjected, "it's done all the time. That's why so many folks use paper shredders these days."

Gil forced himself to take a calming breath, trying to find sense in it all. When he failed, he dropped his elbows to the table and his forehead against his palms. "So what do I do now?"

"I'd think the smart thing to do would be to find her," Dave suggested quietly. "Talk to her. Find out if she really is pregnant. Then decide what you want to do from there."

Gil snapped up his head. "If she *is* pregnant," he said through clenched teeth, "then there's nothing to decide. I'm marrying her."

Dave shared a look with the press agent, but both men remained silent.

Gil had suffered through some bad days in his life, but not one of them came close to matching the gut-wrenching day he'd just experienced. The phones in his office at the capitol and at the mansion had rung incessantly, with reporters wanting a comment from Gil about Suzy's purported pregnancy. In order to avoid the media hounds, he'd finally escaped to his ranch, giving credibility and honesty to his secretary's replies that he was out of town and unavailable for comment.

And when he'd arrived at his ranch, he'd made damn sure *this* time he locked the gate behind him. He didn't want to give any overzealous reporter the opportunity to invade his privacy. Not again. Not when he needed time alone. Time to think. Time to come to grips with all that was happening around him. Time to decide what to do.

He rode his horse for the better part of the afternoon, mulling over the possibility that he could very well be an expectant father. But no matter how many times or ways he played the possibility through his mind, it just wouldn't stick. Not that he objected to becoming a father. He'd always wanted children. But, he'd thought he'd first have a wife.

A wife, he thought again, after returning to the house at dusk. With a sigh he dropped down in an easy chair in his den. He'd always planned to have a wife one day. And he'd thought he'd at last found her when he'd met Suzy. Granted, Suzy was nothing like the woman he'd envisioned marrying. He'd always thought he'd marry someone like his mother. A gentle and unassuming woman who would share his love for his ranch and his views on the world and life in general.

Chuckling, he shook his head, then let it drop back against the chair with a sigh. Suzy was anything but gentle, and she was about as unassuming as a three-ring circus. She was full of sass and vinegar and so colorful that a person needed sunglasses to protect their eyes when they so much as looked her way.

Then why do you miss her so much, he asked himself, when she's nothing at all like the woman you had thought you'd choose as your wife. It's because she *was* different, he admitted, smiling a little at the memories and images that filled his mind. He loved the way she went nose-to-nose with him when they disagreed on a topic, the way she thumbed her nose at convention with her crazy hairdos and even crazier way of dressing. He loved her heart, her smile, her laugh. The way she walked. The way she talked. The way she curled up against him when they slept together. Hell, he couldn't think of anything about her he didn't love.

Which made him realize that he couldn't let her go. Not without putting up a fight. He couldn't just sit back and allow her to walk out of his life. Not when he wanted her with him. Beside him. Always. And he wanted their child. The one she carried, but had kept secret from him.

At the thought, he narrowed his eyes, the missing pieces of the confusing puzzle finally slipping into place. He might not know *how* she got pregnant, but he sure as hell knew *why* she hadn't told him about the baby, and he understood, too, why she'd run away. She was trying to protect him, his career and reputation, just as she'd tried to protect him from her sordid past by refusing to see him.

And a woman who chose to sacrifice so much just

to protect a man's reputation did so for only one reason. She did it for love.

Closing his eyes, he relaxed for the first time that day, his mind made up. Tomorrow he was starting his search again.

And when he found her, this time he was proposing.

"Hey, Governor!"

Gil paused on the steps of the capitol and turned to find a young reporter running to catch up with him, followed closely behind by a cameraman with a camcorder before his face. "Yes?"

The reporter pushed a wireless mike at Gil. "Is it true that you're going to be a father?"

"I'd rather not comment on that at the moment." He turned away and continued up the steps.

"I heard she ditched you," the reporter called after him. "Would you like to comment on that?"

Gil stopped at the verbal jab, then turned slowly back around. "Yes. As a matter of fact, I would like to comment on that, though I don't believe she ditched *me*," he added, taking a menacing step down toward the reporter. "I believe she ditched *you* and all those like you. She doesn't particularly care for the media, nor having her life played out on the front page of every newspaper and television screen in the state."

He took another step down the stairs, his eyes narrowed on the reporter. "What's your name?"

"Gary. Gary Whitaker."

"Well, Gary, let me ask you a question. How do you think you would like it if every move you made was recorded for all the world to see or read about? If every time you walked out your door, there was somebody there waiting to flash a camera in your face or stick a microphone down your throat? How would you like it if every time you kissed your wife or girlfriend or had a spat with her, the world saw it on television or read about it in the paper the next day?"

Scowling, the young reporter lowered the microphone. "Kill the camera, Joe. There's no story here."

Gil kept his gaze on the reporter. "No. Keep rolling, Joe," he said to the cameraman. "Your buddy here asked me a question and I gave him an answer. An honest one. But he doesn't seem to want to answer the one I asked him." He narrowed his eyes. "I wonder why?"

The public's response to Suzy's disappearance was surprising...and heartwarming. Billboards and bumper stickers started appearing around Austin and throughout the state with words of encouragement. Though the messages they carried varied, the sentiments were all the same. It seemed the folks in Texas supported Gil's right to a private life and wanted him to bring Suzy home to the governor's mansion.

Gil saw a minimum of ten bumper stickers on the drive to Elgin, all carrying the same message: Go Get Her, Guv! And that's exactly what he planned to do, he told himself as he knocked on the front door of Suzy's mother's house. Though Dave had assured him that it was just a matter of time before he was able to track Suzy down, Gil was tired of waiting. If anyone knew where Suzy was, it would be her mother. Suzy felt too big a responsibility for her mother to leave without telling her how she could be reached, which was why Gil had decided to talk to Ms. Crane again. Only, this time in person.

''Who's there?'' a voice called from the other side of the door.

''Gil Riley, ma'am. I wondered if I could talk to you for a moment.''

There was a rattle of chain and the door opened a crack. ''If you're looking for Suzy, I've already told you she isn't here.''

''No, ma'am. I didn't come to see Suzy. I came to see you.''

The door opened a little wider, and Gil got his first look at Suzy's mother. The resemblance between mother and daughter was faint, but there, as was the same wariness he'd seen Suzy exhibit so many times.

After hesitating a moment longer, she opened the door and allowed him to enter. She quickly closed it behind him and slipped the security chain into place, then motioned for him to follow her into the living room.

She gestured to the sofa, then sat opposite him in a wing chair. ''Why did you want to see me?''

''To talk to you about Suzy, ma'am,'' he said and pulled off his hat. ''I need to see her, Ms. Crane. Talk to her. And I know that you're the only one who can tell me where she is.''

She wrung her hands. "She made me promise not to tell anyone. Especially you."

Gil leaned forward, bracing his forearms on his knees and holding his hat between his hands. "I know this is difficult for you, Ms. Crane. And I respect your desire to honor the promise you made to Suzy, but it's really important that I talk to her." He bent his head and stared at his hat as he turned it slowly in his hands. "I didn't know she was pregnant, Ms. Crane. She didn't tell me. But I do know why she's run away. She's trying to protect me. But I don't want her protection. I want her. I love her," he said quietly, then looked up, unashamed of the emotion that choked him. "I love her with all my heart, and I'll love our baby, too."

He watched the tears rush to her eyes, and he slipped off the sofa to drop down on a knee before her, gathering her hand in his. "I swear by all that's good and merciful that I'm not here to bring any more embarrassment or pain to your daughter. All I want is a chance to talk to her. The opportunity to tell her that I love her. That I want to marry her. And that I'll do whatever is necessary to protect her."

She squeezed her fingers around his as tears ran down her cheeks. "My daughter's a very lucky young lady to have as fine a man as you love her."

"No, ma'am," he said, shaking his head. "I'm the lucky one. Suzy's the best thing that's ever happened to me."

She drew in a long breath. "All right. I'll tell you

where she is. But first you must promise me something."

Gil gripped her hand more tightly in his. "Anything."

"Don't accept no for an answer." She laughed softly at his surprised look and pulled her hand from his to blot at her cheeks. "I know my daughter, Governor. She won't give in easily. Especially when she thinks that in doing so she might harm you in some way. She'll fight and kick at you every step of the way."

Smiling for the first time in what felt like weeks, Gil stood and settled his hat over his head. "To tell you the truth, Ms. Crane," he said with a wink, "I'm hoping she does kick up a fuss. I've been hankering for a good fight for over a week."

Nine

"You know where the place is, don't you?"

"Yes, Gil," Dave replied patiently. "I mapped out the route before we left the mansion."

Gil shifted nervously in the seat. "How much further?"

Dave rolled his eyes. "Would you relax? We'll get there when we get there."

Gil dragged off his hat and wiped at the perspiration beading his forehead. "I never should have let you talk me into driving me there. I should have driven myself."

"And picked up a fistful of speeding tickets along the way," Dave muttered. "Come on, Gil. Relax. I'll get you there in plenty of time."

At the mention of time Gil glanced at the clock on

the dash. "I told the press that I'd be there by seven tonight."

"And you will be," Dave assured him. "Just sit back and relax."

"If you tell me to relax one more time, I'm going to—"

There was a loud *pop* and the black sedan veered sharply to the left.

Gil sat up straight. "What was that? What are you doing?" he shouted as Dave slowed and steered the car onto the shoulder.

"A blowout," Dave replied, frowning. "We've got a flat tire."

Gil was out of the car before it completely stopped and was lifting the trunk lid, which Dave had popped.

"I'll change it," Dave said, nudging Gil out of his way. "You don't want to get yourself dirty."

Scowling, Gil grabbed a flashlight from the trunk.

"I don't need any light," Dave told him. "I can see well enough to change the tire."

"I'm not getting the flashlight to hold for you," Gil snapped. "I'm getting it so I can try to flag down a passing car."

Shaking his head, Dave pulled the spare from the trunk and headed for the side of the car. "Whatever you say, boss."

His scowl deepening, Gil switched on the flashlight and stomped to the side of the interstate. As a car approached, he waved the flashlight, swearing when the car kept going. Another vehicle approached, and

Gil stepped out onto the highway, waving the flash-light wildly.

The car slowed, then pulled onto the shoulder. Gil ran for the vehicle as the driver rolled down his window.

"Thank you for stopping, sir," Gil said breathlessly. "We had a blowout, and it's imperative that I get to Dallas before seven. By any chance are you headed that way?"

The gnarled old man driving the car turned to look at his wife in the passenger seat. "Well, yeah," the old man said. "As a matter of fact, me and my wife are going to visit our grandkids there."

The man's wife leaned across the seat to peer up at Gil, and her eyes widened in surprise. "Why, Papa! It's the governor!"

The old man squinted his eyes and gave Gil a closer look. "Well, damned if it ain't," he sputtered, and pushed open the door. He stuck out his hand. "Reed Fisher, Governor. It's a pleasure to meet you."

Gil pumped the man's hand. "A pleasure to meet you, too, Mr. Fisher. Now about that ride…"

"Sure 'nuf," the old man said, and opened the back door. "Climb right on in."

"Dave!" Gil called as he ducked into the back seat of the couple's car. "Come on. I've got us a ride."

Already busy changing the flat, Dave dropped the tire iron and swiped his hands down the seat of his slacks as he hustled toward the car. He climbed in next to Gil just as the old man started up the car again.

"We sure do appreciate this," Gil said as the old man pulled back out onto the highway.

The woman twisted around and offered her hand over the seat. "I'm Mary Ruth," she said, smiling shyly, "but all my friends call me Mimi."

Gil shook her hand. "Pleased to meet you, ma'am."

Dave nodded politely. "Ma'am."

Papa, as Mimi had called her husband, glanced in the rearview mirror at Gil. "Whatcha headed to Dallas for, Governor?"

"Papa," Mimi scolded. "The governor's activities are none of your business."

Gil snorted a laugh. "I wish everyone shared your view, Mimi. Especially the press."

She made a tsking sound with her tongue. "The things they put in the paper these days. Why, in my day, they wouldn't have dared print such derogatory things about a man in your position."

"I appreciate your opinion, Mimi," Gil replied. "It's just a shame more people don't share it." He leaned to peer anxiously at the road ahead. "We're heading for a restaurant on Greenville Avenue, Mr. Fisher. Jon's Place. Have you heard of it?"

"No. Can't say that I have. But give me the address and I'll bet I can find it."

Gil settled back in his seat, nervously rubbing his hands down his thighs as Dave rattled off the address and basic directions to reach the restaurant.

"I think it's a crime the things the press wrote

about that woman you've been seeing," Mimi said. "Suzy was her name, wasn't it?"

Gil nodded. "Yes, ma'am. In fact, I'm on my way right now to see her."

She twisted around in the seat, her eyes rounding. "You're going after her?"

"Yes, ma'am, I am. And I'm not leaving until she agrees to marry me."

Mimi turned back around and reached to pat her husband on the knee. "How romantic," she said, sighing dreamily.

"If you'd like," Gil invited, "you two can hang around and see how things go."

"Oh, we couldn't," Mimi said, shaking her head. "A marriage proposal is a private thing and not meant to be intruded upon by strangers."

Dave dropped back his head and laughed. "Not this one," he said, still chuckling. "The governor's invited the entire press corp to witness *this* proposal."

Jon pushed his way through the swinging door and into the kitchen, carrying a tray loaded with dirty glasses, his face flushed from exertion. "Where in the hell are these people coming from?" he asked breathlessly as he slid the tray onto an empty spot on the counter.

Suzy swiped at the perspiration on her brow as she flipped an order of quesadillas on the grill. "Is that a complaint?"

"Hell, no!" Jon said, grinning. "Business hasn't been this good since opening night."

Suzy shoved a tray loaded with plates of nachos toward him. "If you want to make sure it stays that way, take these to table four. Marcy's swamped and hasn't had time."

"Sure thing," Jon said, and scooped up the tray, holding it above his head as he pushed through the swinging door.

Squinting up at the computer screen of orders, Suzy wiped her hands on her apron as she checked what was up next. "Quesadillas again," she muttered wearily. "Don't these people eat anything but Tex-Mex?"

Pausing a moment to stretch the kinks from her back, she sighed and reached for a stack of tortillas and laid them out on the grill. Just as she scooped up a spatula of grilled strips of onion and green peppers to spread across the tortillas, a shout came from the other side of the door, followed by loud cheers and clapping.

Curious to know what all the commotion was about, Suzy set aside the spatula and crossed to the door to peek through the glass. People stood five deep in front of it, blocking her view. Frustrated, she pushed open the door and slipped into the small dining room, rising to the balls of her feet and straining to see over the people who stood in front of her.

Unable to see anything but the backs of heads, she pushed her way through the crowd, but finally gave up and nudged the man standing beside her. "What's going on?" she asked.

He glanced down. "It's the governor," he shouted

to make himself heard over the din. "Gil Riley just walked in."

Suzy's stomach dropped to her feet, then bounced up to crowd her throat. "The governor?" she repeated sickly. "Here?"

"Yeah, he—"

But Suzy was already turning away. She didn't need to hear more. Gil was here? she thought hysterically. Oh, God! She had to get out of there!

She'd almost made it back to the kitchen's swinging door when a hand closed around her arm.

"Suzy. Wait."

She stopped, squeezing her eyes shut at the sound of the familiar drawl. "Gil, please," she begged, and tried to tug free.

He tightened his grip. "If I could have everyone's attention," he shouted to the crowd.

Voices died in a wave that rolled outward until the entire restaurant was as quiet as a church at prayer time.

"I'm sure most of you came here out of curiosity," he said in a voice that carried to the far corners of the room.

A few mumbled comments and spurts of laughter followed his announcement.

He raised a hand for silence. "And others came knowing what to expect," he added, and smiled at an elderly couple Suzy saw standing by Dave at the front of the crowd.

"The reason I called this press conference," he

continued, ''is to set the record straight once and for all.''

He dragged a reluctant Suzy forward and wrapped an arm around her shoulders, forcing her to stand at his side. ''I know a lot of you have wondered about the mysterious woman in my life.''

More mumbled comments and jeers followed. Gil waited until the room was quiet again.

''Well, here she is.'' He looked down at Suzy and smiled. ''Miss Suzy Crane.''

''Gil, please,'' she whispered frantically, trying to duck from beneath his arm. ''You don't know what you're doing.''

''Yeah, I do.'' With his gaze on hers, he slipped his arm from around her and turned to face her, catching both of her hands in his before she could escape. ''As most of you know,'' he said to the crowd, ''Suzy and I met about a month ago. And this may sound trite, but as far as I'm concerned, it was love at first sight.''

''Gil, please!'' she begged, near tears.

''Unfortunately,'' he continued, ignoring her, ''any chance of us having a normal relationship was hindered by...'' He sent a telling look to the crowd of people watching. ''Well, let's just say my position as governor cast a spotlight on our relationship that most couples are spared.''

He looked back down at Suzy, and his smile returned, the warmth and encouragement in it reaching into her heart and twisting painfully.

''Gil,'' she pleaded, desperate to make him listen.

"And I regret that," he said, his eyes softening in apology as he gazed down at her. "Not for myself. But for Suzy. No one deserves the beating she's taken from the press because of her association with me. And no woman should be deprived the romance normally associated with falling in love, just because the man she's involved with is the state governor. Isn't that right, Mimi?" he asked.

"You're darn right it is!" the elderly lady standing by Dave replied indignantly.

Gil went on. "There's not much I can do about what's happened in the past, but I want everyone in this room to know how much this lady standing in front of me means to me." He paused a moment and gave Suzy's hands a reassuring squeeze. "Even if it means giving up the office of governor to get all of you to leave her alone, to keep her name out of the headlines, then that's what I'm prepared to do."

Suzy's gasp was like an explosion in the silent room. "Gil!" she cried, trying to jerk her hands free. "No! You can't! I won't let you!"

He tossed back his head and laughed. "Did you hear that?" he shouted to the crowd. "She says she won't let me quit." As he gazed down at her, the laughter slowly faded from his eyes. "But I will, Suzy," he said quietly. "If that's what it takes to keep from losing you, I'd walk away from the governor's mansion and never look back."

"Gil..."

"I love you, Suzy," he said firmly. "But I won't see you hurt anymore. And I won't sacrifice what we have together for a public office. If it comes to a choice, I want you to know I'll always choose you every time.''

"Hey, governor!" someone shouted from the far side of the room. "Can we quote you on that?"

"You're damn right you can!" Gil yelled.

"What about the rumor that she's pregnant?" someone else called. "Can you verify that for us?"

His gaze turning tender as he continued to look down at Suzy, Gil swept a strand of damp hair from her cheek. "Are you?" he asked softly.

Choked by tears, Suzy could only nod.

A smile slowly spread across his face. "Yes," he reported for all to hear. "She's definitely pregnant. And for the record," he added proudly, "the baby's mine."

"Does this mean you're getting married?" a female voice asked.

Mimi turned to look at the woman in exasperation. "For heaven's sake! Give the man time!" She turned back around and pushed a hand at Gil, urging him to continue. "Go on, honey," she said kindly. "Say what you came here to say."

Gil inhaled deeply. "Suzy," he said, releasing the breath with her name. "Will you—"

"Wait!" Mimi cried, and rushed forward. She quickly untied the apron from around Suzy's waist and lifted it over her head. "A woman receiving a proposal wants to look her best," she fussed gently as she straightened Suzy's collar and fluffed her hair.

Satisfied, she stepped back and smiled. "Now we're ready, Governor."

Gil bit back a smile. "Are you sure?"

Blushing, Mimi fisted the apron at her waist. "Positive."

Taking Suzy's hands again, Gil sank down to a knee, his gaze on hers. "I know this probably isn't the way you'd choose to hear what I have to say. But I think it's important for everyone here, as well as those who will read or hear about this later, to understand how I truly feel about you. From the day we first met, you captured my heart, my soul. But what I felt for you then was nothing compared to what I feel for you now."

He paused and swallowed hard, suddenly choked by emotion. "I love you, Suzy," he whispered, giving her hands a squeeze. "I love you with all my heart and will until the day I die. And I will love the baby we've made together and will protect it with my life, just as I promise to protect you."

He paused again, his face somber, his eyes filled with hope. "Suzy Crane, will you honor me by agreeing to become my wife?"

Her lips trembling uncontrollably, Suzy sank to her knees before him. "Yes," she whispered and reached to cup his face. "Yes," she said again, smiling through her tears as she drew his face to hers.

Cheers erupted around them as their lips met, and bits of shredded napkin were thrown in the air to rain down over them as they hugged, laughing.

Drawing away, Gil stood, pulling Suzy to her feet,

as well. With his gaze on hers, he drew her into his arms again. "I love you," he whispered.

Her fingers trembling, Suzy gathered his face between her hands and looked deeply into his eyes. "And I love you."

He kissed her again, more passionately this time, while holding her tightly against his chest, their hearts beating as one.

"Hey!" someone shouted. "Are we invited to the wedding?"

"You're damn right you are," Gil replied, leaning back to beam a smile at his bride-to-be. "The whole damn state is going to be invited to this wedding, aren't they, darlin'?"

Suzy arched a brow. "On one condition," she replied, then turned to peer at the crowd of reporters gathered. "They have to bring the beer."

Gil tossed back his head and laughed. "That's my Suzy!"

*   *   *   *   *

Silhouette®

Desire.

welcomes you to

20 AMBER COURT

Four twentysomething women work together, share an address... and confide in each other as they fall in love!

Join Jayne, Lila, Meredith and Sylvie as they face new challenges in business...and romance.

On sale September 2001:
WHEN JAYNE MET ERIK
by bestselling author
Elizabeth Bevarly (SD#1389)

On sale October 2001:
SOME KIND OF INCREDIBLE
by popular author
Katherine Garbera (SD#1395)

On sale November 2001:
THE BACHELORETTE
by rising star
Kate Little (SD#1401)

On sale December 2001:
RISQUÉ BUSINESS
by award-winning author
Anne Marie Winston (SD#1407)

Available at your favorite retail outlet.

Silhouette®
Where love comes alive™

Visit Silhouette at www.eHarlequin.com

SD20AC

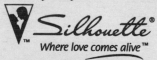

CALL THE ONES YOU LOVE OVER THE HOLIDAYS!

Save $25 off future book purchases when you buy any four Harlequin® or Silhouette® books in October, November and December 2001,

PLUS

receive a phone card good for 15 minutes of long-distance calls to anyone you want in North America!

WHAT AN INCREDIBLE DEAL!

Just fill out this form and attach 4 proofs of purchase (cash register receipts) from October, November and December 2001 books, and Harlequin Books will send you a coupon booklet worth a total savings of $25 off future purchases of Harlequin® and Silhouette® books, AND a 15-minute phone card to call the ones you love, anywhere in North America.

Please send this form, along with your cash register receipts as proofs of purchase, to:
In the USA: Harlequin Books, P.O. Box 9057, Buffalo, NY 14269-9057
In Canada: Harlequin Books, P.O. Box 622, Fort Erie, Ontario L2A 5X3
Cash register receipts must be dated no later than December 31, 2001.
Limit of 1 coupon booklet and phone card per household.
Please allow 4-6 weeks for delivery.

I accept your offer! Please send me my coupon booklet and a 15-minute phone card:

Name: _____

Address: _____ City: _____

State/Prov.: _____ Zip/Postal Code: _____

Account Number (if available): _____

---

097 KJB DAGL
PHQ4012

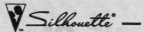

where love comes alive—online...

eHARLEQUIN.com

shop eHarlequin

♥ Find all the new Silhouette releases at everyday great discounts.

♥ Try before you buy! Read an excerpt from the latest Silhouette novels.

♥ Write an online review and share your thoughts with others.

reading room

♥ Read our Internet exclusive daily and weekly online serials, or vote in our interactive novel.

♥ Talk to other readers about your favorite novels in our Reading Groups.

♥ Take our Choose-a-Book quiz to find the series that matches you!

authors' alcove

♥ Find out interesting tidbits and details about your favorite authors' lives, interests and writing habits.

♥ Ever dreamed of being an author? Enter our Writing Round Robin. The Winning Chapter will be published online! Or review our writing guidelines for submitting your novel.

All this and more available at
www.eHarlequin.com
on Women.com Networks

SINTB1R

If you enjoyed what you just read,
then we've got an offer you can't resist!

Take 2 bestselling love stories FREE!

Plus get a FREE surprise gift!

Clip this page and mail it to Silhouette Reader Service™

IN U.S.A.
3010 Walden Ave.
P.O. Box 1867
Buffalo, N.Y. 14240-1867

IN CANADA
P.O. Box 609
Fort Erie, Ontario
L2A 5X3

YES! Please send me 2 free Silhouette Desire® novels and my free surprise gift. After receiving them, if I don't wish to receive anymore, I can return the shipping statement marked cancel. If I don't cancel, I will receive 6 brand-new novels every month, before they're available in stores! In the U.S.A., bill me at the bargain price of $3.34 plus 25¢ shipping and handling per book and applicable sales tax, if any*. In Canada, bill me at the bargain price of $3.74 plus 25¢ shipping and handling per book and applicable taxes**. That's the complete price and a savings of at least 10% off the cover prices—what a great deal! I understand that accepting the 2 free books and gift places me under no obligation ever to buy any books. I can always return a shipment and cancel at any time. Even if I never buy another book from Silhouette, the 2 free books and gift are mine to keep forever.

225 SEN DFNS
326 SEN DFNT

Name	(PLEASE PRINT)	
Address	Apt.#	
City	State/Prov.	Zip/Postal Code

* Terms and prices subject to change without notice. Sales tax applicable in N.Y.
** Canadian residents will be charged applicable provincial taxes and GST.
All orders subject to approval. Offer limited to one per household and not valid to current Silhouette Desire® subscribers.
® are registered trademarks of Harlequin Enterprises Limited.

DES01   ©1998 Harlequin Enterprises Limited

Revitalize!

With help from
Silhouette's *New York Times*
bestselling authors
and receive a

FREE

Refresher Kit!
Retail Value of $25.00 U.S.

LUCIA IN LOVE by Heather Graham
and LION ON THE PROWL by Kasey Michaels

LOVE SONG FOR A RAVEN by Elizabeth Lowell
and THE FIVE-MINUTE BRIDE by Leanne Banks

MACKENZIE'S PLEASURE by Linda Howard
and DEFENDING HIS OWN by Beverly Barton

DARING MOVES by Linda Lael Miller
and MARRIAGE ON DEMAND by Susan Mallery

Don't miss out!

*Look for this exciting promotion, on sale in
October 2001 at your favorite retail outlet.
See inside books for details.*

Only from

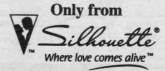

Visit Silhouette at www.eHarlequin.com   PSNCP-POPR

THE FORTUNES of TEXAS

invite you to a memorable Christmas celebration in

Gifts of FORTUNE

Patriarch Ryan Fortune has met death head-on and now he has a special gift for each of the four honorable individuals who stood by him in his hour of need. This holiday collection contains stories by three of your most beloved authors.

THE HOLIDAY HEIR
by Barbara Boswell

THE CHRISTMAS HOUSE
by Jennifer Greene

MAGGIE'S MIRACLE
by Jackie Merritt

And be sure to watch for **Did You Say Twins?!** by Maureen Child, the exciting conclusion to the *Fortunes of Texas: The Lost Heirs* miniseries, coming only to Silhouette Desire in December 2001.

Don't miss these unforgettable romances... available at your favorite retail outlet.

Silhouette®
Where love comes alive™

Visit Silhouette at www.eHarlequin.com

PSGOF

Silhouette Books cordially invites you to come
on down to Jacobsville, Texas, for

DIANA PALMER's
LONG, TALL TEXAN
Weddings

(On sale November 2001)

The LONG, TALL TEXANS series from international
bestselling author Diana Palmer is cherished around the
world. Now three sensuous, charming love stories from
this blockbuster series—*Coltrain's Proposal, Beloved* and
"Paper Husband"—are available in one special volume!

*As free as wild mustangs, Jeb, Simon and Hank vowed
never to submit to the reins of marriage. Until, of course,
a certain trio of provocative beauties tempt these Lone Star
lovers off the range...and into a tender, timeless embrace!*

You won't want to miss
LONG, TALL TEXAN WEDDINGS
by Diana Palmer, featuring two
full-length novels and one short story!

Available only from Silhouette Books at your favorite retail outlet.

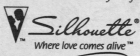

Silhouette®
™ *Where love comes alive*™

Visit Silhouette at www.eHarlequin.com   PSLTTW

presents an exciting new miniseries by reader favorite

LEANNE BANKS

Each member of this royal family finds the love
of a commoner to be most uncommon of all!

ROYAL DAD—SD #1400, on sale November 2001

Handsome Prince Michel Philippe has more than he
bargained for when feisty American Maggie Gillian
descends on his kingdom to tutor his little son...
and melts this single dad's hardened heart!

Watch for more tantalizing tales of
"The Royal Dumonts" in 2002!
Only from Silhouette Desire.

Available at your favorite retail outlet.

Where love comes alive™

Visit Silhouette at www.eHarlequin.com   SDRD